Other Avon Camelot Books by
Marie G. Lee

IF IT HADN'T BEEN FOR YOON JUN
NIGHT OF THE CHUPACABRAS

P9-CRX-556

F is for Fabulo

F IS FOR FABULOSO

金

Marie G. Lee

AN AVON CAMELOT BOOK

Acknowledgments

Special thanks to Youngmi Cho and Holly Kim for helping me with my research.

—Marie G. Lee

F is for Fabuloso

1

Jin-Ha Kim didn't know yarn could be so beautiful.

It was the color of a summer's night sky. It looked so inviting that she couldn't help plunging both hands into the bin. The yarn surrounded her fingers like the world's softest mittens.

Jin-Ha looked over at her mother, whose eye was also caught by the yarn. Jin-Ha's heart quickened. Maybe the beautiful yarn would do it. Maybe it could break the spell caused by that awful memory long enough so her mother could speak. Boldly. In English.

Maybe.

"We just got that yarn in—it's a new color," said a silver-haired lady who was entering the store from a back room. She smiled, her cheeks like baked apples.

"Isn't it beautiful?" she asked, as she began to

straighten a display of knitting magazines whose covers boasted healthy-looking blue-eyed people wearing sweaters and knit hats. This lady seemed nice, Jin-Ha thought. Not at all like the bad man in line at the bank . . .

They'd been in America maybe three weeks and had gone to the bank to get change for the laundry machine. The teller hadn't understood Jin-Ha's mother's request for a roll of quarters, but before she could repeat herself, the man in line behind them had grumbled, "Learn English!" in a voice *everyone* could hear.

Jin-Ha's mother *had* been speaking in English. Her pronunciation might have sounded more like "a row of quartahs, prease-oo" than "a roll of quarters, please," but that didn't excuse the man's behavior. Jin-Ha was surprised that no one had reprimanded this man's rudeness—the teller had even chuckled a little bit. What kind of a place was America? In Korea no one would ever say "Learn Korean!" to an American. In fact, if an American spoke *any* Korean, they would probably all be *amazed*. . . .

But from that day on, her mother began to fear speaking English, and in public, she mostly asked Jin-Ha to do the talking for her. Jin-Ha didn't mind. But she did worry about what would happen when she left to go to college. She was only in the seventh grade, but she still worried. What if her mother never learned to speak English?

Jin-Ha glanced at her mother. *You can do it*, she thought. *The lady asked you an easy question: "Isn't the yarn beautiful?" You could answer back: "Oh, yes, this yarn is beautiful."*

2

Just as the silence was beginning to press on everyone, Jin Ha's mother told her in Korean, *"Ask her how much the yarn is."*

Jin-Ha let out her breath. Not this time.

"How much is this yarn?"

"It's three dollars and twenty-five cents a skein."

"It's three twenty-five per unit," she told her mother.

Her mother reached out and stroked the yarn as if it were a purring navy-blue cat.

"Hm, that's kind of expensive," she said to Jin-Ha. *"But I think it could make a nice-looking sweater for your father."*

"A very nice sweater," Jin-Ha agreed. *"And navy blue is his favorite color."*

"If I work hard, I could even get it done before Christmas. Your poor father always seems to be so cold."

He's not the only one, Jin-Ha wanted to say. Norbuhl, Minnesota was much colder than Korea. Its winters sent down mountains of snow and freezing winds that made their windowpanes shiver while the snowflakes whirled outside.

And the floors were freezing cold. In Korea, they'd had warm floors—oiled rice paper floors heated from the bottom. Sleeping and sitting on these floors made you forget about any cold outside. Jin-Ha was sure their apartment wouldn't feel half so cold if they had warm floors here.

"Are you going to buy it?" she asked her mother.

"Yes," her mother said, bouncing a bundle of yarn in her hand, testing its weight. *"Tell her we'll need eleven of those."*

"Okay, we'll take it. We'll need eleven . . . um, what did you call those?" Jin-Ha pointed to the pile of yarn.

3

"Skeins," the lady said, stretching the word until it came out in three syllables: "*Skay-in-zzzz*." She held up some yarn that had been taken from the loose skeins and rolled into a ball.

"And this is a ball. *Ba-awll*." Jin-Ha sighed. *Ball* was easy—it was one of the first words everyone learned!

Jin-Ha turned to her mother. "*A bundle of yarn is called a* skein *in English*," she said, and her mother nodded.

"What are you going to make?" the lady asked, peering over her tiny half-glasses at Jin-Ha's mother. A lot of times when Jin-Ha was translating, people ignored her mother as if she, and not Jin-Ha, were the child, which made Jin-Ha mad. After all, it was her mother who was doing the speaking. Jin-Ha was just putting the English in her words.

But this lady was very respectful. Jin-Ha glanced at her mother, positive she understood her words: What. Are. You. Going. To. Make. But her mother stayed silent and nudged her with her elbow, Jin-Ha's cue to answer for her.

"She's making a sweater for my father," Jin-Ha said.

"How nice! Let me go get the rest of your yarn." The lady disappeared behind a bright orange curtain decorated with snoozing cats.

Jin-Ha's mother walked over to a wall to see the knitted things pinned up there: wild-colored winter hats, scarves with fringe at the end, red-and-green stockings with people's names stitched on them: BRAD, CHRIS, GAIL.

In the center of the display was a beautiful ladies' sweater knit out of the same yarn they were going to use for Jin-Ha's father's sweater, except this yarn was a jewel pink. Jin-Ha's mother touched the sleeve.

"It's soft, I bet," Jin-Ha said.

"Yes, very soft," her mother said, a little dreamily. Jin-Ha liked the high neck—it was like having a built-in scarf. Jin-Ha's mother looked at the price tag hanging off the sleeve and gasped softly. *"It's very expensive to have someone else knit it for you,"* she said.

The lady came out with the rest of the skeins and rang the sale up.

"It should total thirty-five dollars and seventy-five cents," Jin-Ha's mother told her.

"That'll be $35.75," said the lady.

"You're exactly right," Jin-Ha told her mother.

Jin-Ha's mother nodded as she handed the woman the exact amount, down to two quarters, two dimes and a nickel.

The lady handed them a bulging yellow bag with the picture of a mischievous cat tangled up in yarn, with THAT YARN CAT written at the bottom.

"Have fun with your knitting," the lady said, looking Jin-Ha's mother directly in the eye.

Jin-Ha's mother blushed. Jin-Ha hoped she would say something back, a quick "thank you" or at least "good-bye."

She smiled and bowed slightly.

"Good-bye," Jin-Ha said to the lady, a little louder than she meant to.

2

Jin-Ha loved spending time with her mother. No matter
how busy she was with the housework, she always made
time for her only child. In Korea, in the summer, her
mother had picked the petals of the *bongsoon* flower,
crushed them, and spread them on Jin-Ha's fingernails
to tint them pink. In the winter, her mother had braided
Jin-Ha's hair for school while telling her all sorts of Korean folk stories as they sat on the warm floor. Jin-Ha's
favorite was the one about Shim Cheong, the brave girl.

Shim Cheong was an only child, just like Jin-Ha. Her
father was blind and she took care of him because her
mother was dead. One terrible winter they ran out of
food to eat, so she offered herself to some fishermen who
needed a young girl as a sacrifice to the sea to protect
their ship. They gave her a few bags of rice, which she
gave to her father, and Shim Cheong went with the fish-

ermen. When a terrible storm came up, Shim Cheong bravely threw herself into the stormy sea before the frightened fishermen could toss her overboard.

But the best part of the story was that she didn't drown. Instead, she floated down to an undersea kingdom where there were people, like on earth, and where there was air to breathe. Later, she came back to her village as a rich and magical woman, and the first thing she did was cure her father's blindness. Korean parents tell this story in hopes that their children could be a bit like Shim Cheong. Jin-Ha had always wondered if she could ever be that brave.

In America, there were no *bongsoon* flowers, and Jin-Ha's hair was cut in a bob, too short to braid, but her mother still took the time to tell Jin-Ha stories. A lot of the stories started with, "Long, long time ago, back when tigers smoked pipes . . ." It was even more important now to tell her stories, Jin-Ha's mother said, because she didn't want Jin-Ha to forget Korea.

Jin-Ha and her mother had left Korea to follow Jin-Ha's father, who had come to America by himself as a student six years ago. So far they had all been together in America for two years.

Jin-Ha still missed her friends Kyung-Hee and Ji-Sun, and she missed her auntie, *Imo*, and her grandmother, *Halmoni*. She also missed their house with the warm floors and the tiled roof that curved up at the ends like wings.

Adjusting to America hadn't been all easy. She'd been used to Korean people, with their black hair and black eyes, and suddenly she was surrounded by people who were white as ghosts with pale eyes that seemed to go right through their heads. American food also seemed

7

like tasteless mush compared to spicy Korean food. And learning to speak English, American English, had been terrible at first.

But there were good things, too. She had friends like Deanna and Maggie, and she now loved American food, especially hotdogs, spaghetti, and pizza. Also, she could wear whatever she wanted to school and didn't have to wear a drab gray-and-white uniform like she had in Korea.

It seemed like part of Jin-Ha had become American and part of her remained Korean, and she liked that balance. She worried most about her mother because she sometimes seemed sad without people to talk to when Jin-Ha was in school and her father at work. Jin-Ha was sure her mother's fear of English was the only thing holding her back from meeting people.

And it wasn't as if her mother was dumb. On the contrary, she was very smart. She had gone to a prestigious women's college in Korea, and people had always commented on how eloquent and learned her mother's language was. She had even won a poetry contest sponsored by one of Seoul's big newspapers.

But even though she had studied English and could read it, she had never felt she could speak it well. After the man at the bank had made her feel so bad, she'd lost the little confidence she'd had. Korean, then, was the language they used at home, which meant that her mother didn't even *hear* English any more. Jin-Ha worried that without use and practice, her mother's language skills would stiffen and corrode, the way their garden shears had rusted permanently shut, now that they lived in an apartment and no longer had a garden.

"Do you think you can get the sweater done before

Christmas," Jin-Ha asked her mother as they walked home. *"Without Dad seeing?"*

"I can do it," said her mother.

"In English, they say, 'no problem,' " said Jin-Ha. Jin-Ha's mother smiled at her.

"No probl-rem," she said, in a hesitant voice.

"That's perfect," said Jin-Ha. *"You sound just like an American."*

Whenever Jin-Ha thought about ways to help her mother, she just had to remember what it was like for herself. In school in Korea, she'd learned English spelling, grammar, and reading—all on paper, without sound. The few times their teacher had spoken in English, it still sounded like Korean, not the language they heard in American songs and movies.

Their teacher also put little tails on English words. "Yes" was "yes-oo," hard was "hard-oo." But the first thing Jin-Ha noticed when they came to Norbuhl was that Americans—just as in their movies—stopped their words right where they ended. *Yes.* Her father had mastered these quick-stop endings as well. *Yes.*

Jin-Ha had practiced for hours, training herself to stop her tongue at the end of a word and not move it. *Yes.* Sometimes it made her feel like gagging. Adding another puff of air, *yes-oo,* or breaking a word like *film* into two, *fil-lim,* seemed natural and to Jin-Ha sounded nicer, but that wasn't the way they spoke here.

The very day they had moved into their apartment, they had encountered an English problem. Jin-Ha's father was out doing an errand, and Jin-Ha and her mother were getting dinner ready. They had needed a match to light their gas stove, so Jin-Ha's mother had told Jin-Ha to go around the apartment building and ask for a match.

9

Jin-Ha had been excited and nervous—this was the first time she would use her English for real.

"Do you want a match?" she remembered asking Mrs. Hokansson, their neighbor, in her best English. Of course, she knew now she should have said, "Do you *have* a match?" but what she had said had sounded fine to her then.

Mrs. Hokansson had looked puzzled, and had then gone back into the apartment. She returned with a cookie. Jin-Ha had wanted to say, "I want a match, not a cookie," but she had been nervous and stayed with her script. "Do you want a match?" she'd asked again. This time, Mrs. Hokansson had shaken her head and closed the door.

None of their neighbors had understood her. None of them had been mean, or even impatient, but they all ended up shaking their heads and closing their doors.

Jin-Ha had come back, matchless. That night when her father returned, they'd had to eat cold food.

"I can't believe that no one in this building has a match," she remembered him saying.

Since they had come in the middle of the American school year, her parents had enrolled her in classes right away. Jin-Ha's mother had gone with her the first day because her father had to work. Jin-Ha had clutched her mother's hand the whole way to school. Her mother, however, had acted like she did this all the time. She answered the secretary's questions, such as where did they live and when was Jin-Ha's birthday, speaking English just fine.

For the more difficult questions, her mother handed

her Korean-English dictionary to the secretary and asked her to point out the words she was using.

Then, a different lady took Jin-Ha to another room and asked her all sorts of questions—How old are you? Where did you live before you came to Norbuhl? Can you read this?—and Jin-Ha answered them. Later, Jin-Ha realized this woman was probably testing her English, to see if she could keep up with her grade.

Eventually, Jin-Ha had been reunited with her mother, but then the secretary had told Jin-Ha she should go to her class, room 2A, right away. Jin-Ha had been scared, but her mother had reminded her that tigers couldn't eat her if she was inside the school building, and then she left. Of course now Jin-Ha knew there weren't any wild tigers in Norbuhl—or in America at all. But she had admired her mother on that day for being so clever and brave, just like Shim Cheong.

Jin-Ha had tried to be brave like Shim Cheong when she got to class. It was already past noon, and her stomach was growling like thunder. She'd been so nervous that morning she hadn't been able to eat a thing.

It hadn't helped that the students had stared at her as she had walked in, and the teacher, an incredibly tall lady even in flat shoes, had immediately leaned down and said, "Jeet? Jeet?" to Jin-Ha. Jin-Ha hadn't understood, and the lady had kept saying, "Jeet? Jeet?" louder and louder, like a scolding bird—and some of the kids had laughed. Jin-Ha hadn't known what to do, where to go. She had wanted to run home, to her mother, to Korea. But there had been no one to help her.

The teacher had repeated, "Jeet? Jeet?" a few more times, and then she sighed and left Jin-Ha alone.

Later, Jin-Ha realized, the teacher had been asking if

she'd eaten—Did-you-eat?—because it had been lunch-time. She could have understood that. But not *jeet.* Americans not only talked fast, they compressed three words into one. No one said *how-are-you,* they said *how-erya.* How would she ever be able to understand English? she had wondered.

But Jin-Ha had learned. She felt perfectly fine with English now. In fact, she even dreamed in English most nights. But she kept reminding herself of the time she had to struggle to understand and say things in English. It was probably the same for her mother, she just needed more time.

3

Back in the apartment, Jin-Ha's mother hid the yarn behind some blankets in the hall closet. Then she turned the thermostat up a hair and set about making dinner.

Jin-Ha went to her room and opened up her book bag, which was stuffed. For her science class she was doing an extra-credit report on bees, and she'd taken out every library book on the subject that she could find. She also had checked out *Black Beauty*, which she'd read three times already. She wanted to read it again because it was a good story, and because she thought horses were such noble creatures.

Jin-Ha often wished she owned some books. Her parents told her to use the library, because why buy books when you could read them for free? This is what her father had done when he was studying at the university.

Jin-Ha stared at *Black Beauty*, which she'd put on her

shelf. The ebony-black horse looked out from the cover. But a big sticker, NORBUHL PUBLIC LIBRARY, blocked out one of the horse's eyes. She put her hand over the sticker, pretending it was hers. If it was, she would write *Jin-Ha Kim, 321 W. Lund Street, Apt. 41, Norbuhl, MN 55776* inside the front cover.

She sighed and opened *Bees and Their Habitats*, even though she had a ton of homework in math, her least favorite subject this year.

In the kitchen, the phone rang. Jin-Ha's mother picked it up.

"No, no," Jin-Ha heard her mother say nervously. This meant that the caller wasn't her father, but someone who spoke English. Jin-Ha ran to the kitchen, where her mother was already holding the receiver out to her.

"Hello," said a man's voice, smooth as the icing on cake.

"Am I speaking with the lady of the house?" he said.

Jin-Ha was confused. She and her mother were both "ladies," weren't they?

"Mm," she said.

"Ah, good. Do your floors suffer from unsightly dirt and grime? Does it seem that after you vacuum, they get dirty again right away?"

The man's voice was like the voices on TV, the ones that ask what you reach for when you eat too much. Or if you know about an inexpensive way to reduce stomach flab. Or that this denture paste works better than that one. They asked questions that weren't really questions; Jin-Ha waited for the rest.

"I bet you didn't know that most trouble in your house actually occurs from *things you can't see*! You know that dust mites—which are less than point-oh-two microns in diameter—we're talking *microscopic*—might be causing allergic reactions in your family, such as sneezing, watery eyes, morning headaches, and a debilitating sense of fatigue. Do any of you have these symptoms?"

Jin-Ha felt like yawning.

"Being tired," she said.

"So what I'd like to do," the voice went on. "Is to demonstrate for you *free of charge*—absolutely no obligation—our new Vroom-o-luxor vacuum cleaner with its patented micro-pore HEPA-1 filter that will most certainly change the way you care for your house and family. Now, just tell me your address, and we can set up an appointment."

Jin-Ha paused. The voice was very soothing and it sounded trustworthy. But she remembered that her teacher had told them never, ever, to give out their address—or even their name—over the phone to strangers.

"I'm sorry," she said. "I can't give you our address."

There was a pause. A throat clearing. Then the silky voice came back on. "You're sure you're the lady of the house? If you don't mind me saying, you sound a bit young. How about that other woman who answered the phone? Or couldn't I just drop off some brochures?"

"No, thank you," Jin-Ha said. The voice kept going, but once she took the phone away from her ear, the silk disintegrated into buzz and squawk. She put the receiver back in the cradle.

"*Who was that?*" asked her mother, as she cut up some zucchini to make *chun*, vegetables in egg batter.

"*I don't know,*" Jin-Ha said. "*Someone wanted to show us a vacuum cleaner, I think to try to get us to buy it.*"

"*Selling over the phone?*" her mother asked, shaking

15

her head. *"What will they think of next in America? Invading people's homes?"*

America could be a strange place, Jin-Ha agreed. On the street, people just said things like "Good morning" or "Hi" to you even if they weren't a friend or relative! They seemed to think it was fine to act like they knew you when they didn't. When they'd first moved into their apartment, a cheerful lady had come to their door with a basket of soap and potholders and other little gifts for the house. She was from something called the "Welcome Wagon," and even though Jin-Ha's father was the only one who understood her, she had gaily chattered on for an hour, acting like she had known them their whole lives.

The phone rang. Jin-Ha picked it up. She hoped it wasn't the man again.

"Hi, Jin—it's me." It was her friend Deanna. In school, Deanna, Maggie, and Jin-Ha were called the "triangle" because one side was never seen without the other two.

"Hi, Deanna," Jin-Ha replied. "What's up?"

"Well, might you want to go back to the library with Maggie and me tonight?"

"Again?" said Jin-Ha. "We were just there."

"It's actually Maggie's idea." Deanna giggled. "Mrs. Rushmont is making us do a report on a famous person for social studies. I already did mine, but Maggie figures she can do some research and run into that guy she has a crush on at the same time."

Maggie had become boy crazy this year, while Jin-Ha and Deanna gave about as much thought to boys as they did to the socks on their feet: they were there. Jin-

Ha thought that boys in general were bad, like Grant Hartwig, the mean-faced hockey player who had called her a "chink" when she had first started school. Her policy was to avoid boys whenever possible. But going to the library? That was another story.

"I'll have to wait until my dad gets home and ask," said Jin-Ha, who never got sick of going to the library.

4

Dinner was rice and the zucchini *chun*. Her mother had made American rice, the only kind they could buy in Norbuhl. Jin-Ha liked Korean rice better because it stuck together in clumps, perfect to be picked up by chopsticks and wrapped in seaweed or eaten with Korean *kimchi*, pickled spicy cabbage. American rice fell apart with chopsticks, so she had to use a fork.

At least they had *kimchi*. Koreans eat *kimchi* at all three meals, and Jin-Ha didn't think she could live without it, even though she ate cereal and milk for breakfast now, like her friends.

Jin-Ha's mother made their *kimchi* and stored it in huge glass jars that once held dill pickles. She mixed cabbage, onion, red pepper, and garlic in a plastic wash-tub, then put them in the jars to pickle on the windowsill.

                    *   *   *
There was a knock at the door.

"It's me."

Jin-Ha let her father in. He looked tired but glad to be home. His green jumpsuit was spotted with oil, like continents on a map, and his fingers were so black it would take a good effort with a pumice stone to get them pinkly clean again.

To Jin-Ha, it was strange to see her father this way. Back in Korea, he had been a scholar and everyone referred to him as Teacher Kim. Before he was hired at Jack & Don's Auto Body, he had rarely ever worked with his hands—except to touch books and calligraphy brushes. He had been such a good student in Korea that the University of Minnesota had invited him to come and study on scholarship. He decided to do that, then come back to Korea to teach.

What had complicated things was that Jin-Ha's father fell in love with America and decided he wanted to stay there when he was through with school. But he was Korean, not American, and getting something as simple-sounding as a "green card" had meant that he had to work not as a teacher, but as a car mechanic's assistant. Jin Ha knew that somehow, her father's kindhearted boss, Jack, was taking care of this green card business for him. But now her scholar father looked just like those guys with rough hands who'd never gone to college. It was kind of funny, he often said, that he was learning to fix cars when they had never owned one themselves.

"Welcome home," Jin-Ha said, bowing, as she always did. Her father smiled at her and removed his shoes at the door.

"There's something wrong with the latch on the dish-

19

washer," her mother said to her father as he came into the apartment.

"*Is this all the greeting I get coming home from a long day of work?*" Her father was smiling, so Jin-Ha knew he was just kidding. He went over to the dishwasher and moved the latch up and down a few times.

"*It's just a loose screw, I think,*" he said. "*I can fix that for you even before you do the dishes tonight.*"

"*Thank you,*" Jin-Ha's mother said. Ever since Jin-Ha's father had started working at Jack & Don's he had become quite adept at fixing things.

"*Dinner smells good,*" he said, peering at the food.

"*Of course it's good,*" said Jin-Ha. "*Look, kimchi!*"

"*Yes, your mother's kimchi is better than kimchi you can buy at any store,*" said her father. "*She is a kimchi Ph.D.*" Her mother looked at him and her cheeks turned pink.

"How was school today?" Jin-Ha's father asked.

"It was fine," she said. "*I'm doing an extra credit report for my science class,*" she told him, switching to Korean so her mother could also understand. "*It's on bees.*"

"*That's good,*" her father said.

"*When is the report due?*" her mother asked.

"*Not for a few weeks,*" Jin-Ha said. "*But I like to get a head start on it. And by the way, I need some more books. Can I go to the library tonight?*"

"*I'm sorry,*" her father said. "*I need to go out until late, and I don't want you walking to the library at night.*"

"*Where do you need to go?*" asked Jin-Ha's mother.

"*My class,*" he said. "*Remember, I said I was going to take a class?*"

"*What class?*"

"*My teacher certification class.*"

"Oh, I didn't know you were going to start it so soon."

"What kind of class is that?" Jin-Ha asked. "You look kind of old to be a student," she teased.

Her father's eyes twinkled. "It's never too late to learn new things," he said. "I'm taking a class that will help me become a teacher."

"Wow, so you can finally become a college professor?"

"A community college professor, perhaps," he said. "Or a high school teacher."

"That's great," Jin-Ha said. "Don't worry about me, I can study at home just fine."

"We haven't really discussed this, this taking a class," Jin-Ha's mother.

"It's a good class," her father said. "And it doesn't cost much."

"But with our budget so tight—"

"Don't worry," he said confidently. "Have I ever let you down?"

"No," she admitted.

"I can't go—my father doesn't have time to walk with me," Jin-Ha told Deanna on the phone. "Do you mind looking to see if there are any more books on bees?"

"Wait, I'll see if my mom will give us a ride," Deanna said. "—Mom! Can you give Jin-Ha and me and Maggie a ride to the library tonight?" Jin-Ha heard Deanna's mom yelling something back.

"She said she can," Deanna said breathlessly. "See you at seven."

5

At night, the brightly lit Norbuhl Public Library looked particularly warm and inviting.

"Wow." Maggie giggled, flipping her gold-red hair. "This is so exciting." Jin-Ha could smell Maggie's perfume, Sweet Memories.

The girls went to their favorite table by the windows and the READING WEEK display and put their coats on the chairs. There were a lot of kids from the junior high here, and even some high school kids.

Deanna unpacked her books and started right in on her homework. Maggie went to find some books on Annie Oakley for her report.

Jin-Ha opened the notebook containing her report on bees. Her last extra-credit report had been on ants. She was fascinated with animals that could live crowded into one place and get along. Her science teacher, Mr. Feron, had told her she didn't need any more extra credit reports—she had over 100 points already—but she liked learning more.

Tonight, like most nights, she also had a ton of math homework, but that heavy book was at the bottom of her bag and she wasn't in the mood to dig it out. Instead, she browsed the card catalog and found another book, *The Society of Bees*, that looked promising. She went upstairs into the stacks to find it.

In the stacks, right by where she thought the book would be, a boy in a blue NORBUHL BLUEJACKETS HOCKEY jacket was leaning against the shelves. She saw that he was reading not a library book, but their huge orange math book, *Concepts of Math II*. The boy looked up. It was Grant Hartwig, the boy who had called her names.

Jin-Ha gulped. But before she could move, he thunked his book shut, glared at her, and ran downstairs.

Jin-Ha was relieved to see *The Society of Bees* on the shelf.

Back at their table, Maggie was hopping around on her chair like a Mexican jumping bean on a hot frying pan.

"Oh, he is just so fabuloso, isn't he?" she was saying to Deanna. *Fabuloso* was Maggie's new word. When she acquired a new word, she used it until she wore it out like an old shoe. Fabuloso was only a week old, but already certain boys (of course) were fabuloso, Sammy's pizza was fabuloso, her cat Playdough was fabuloso, flowered wallpaper was fabuloso, and Jimmie the Twerp, her little brother, was most definitely non-fabuloso for his tendency to come into her room and swat his chocolate-stained hands on her posters of Garry Thunderbird and his band (what else?) The Fabulosos, who had started the craze in the first place.

"Who's fabuloso?" inquired Jin-Ha, as she came back to the table.

"Joel Carlson," Maggie said, pointing. There were a bunch of boys standing by the library's computer. They all had on blue jackets that said NORBUHL JUNIOR HIGH BANTAM A in elaborate embroidery on the front and NOR-BUHL BLUEJACKETS HOCKEY on the back. The hockey players were the most talked-about kids in school. In Korea, some college and high school athletes became quite popular during certain seasons, but here in Minnesota, hockey players—even middle school hockey players—were popular year round.

Beeps and whistles flew out of the computer, along with the hockey players' grunts and rat-tat-tat laughter. Grant Hartwig had joined the crowd. He was a head taller than the other boys, and he was laughing the loudest. In a minute, the librarian was going to come out and say "Shhh." Jin-Ha hated it when people were noisy in the library. It was so disrespectful, and you were supposed to use the computer for research, not games.

"Isn't he fabuloso-ly cute?" Maggie said, not taking her eyes off Joel for a second, as if she were afraid he'd disappear. "And there's the other one, Grant Hartwig. His father is the coach of the high school hockey team, and his brother is Joe Hartwig, that famous hockey player."

Jin-Ha shrugged. She wasn't exactly sure which one in the blue crowd was Joel Carlson. To her, the hockey players were a single many-legged blue animal that talked loudly in class, threw things in the lunchroom, and picked on the smaller kids in murder ball—and somehow, all the boy-crazy girls thought they were the best boys in school.

"Maggie," Deanna said, glancing at the clock on the wall, "it's almost eight o'clock. Don't you think you might want to read a little about Annie Oakley? Look at how much you've done in all this time!"

Maggie looked down on at her paper. So far she had written two whole words: (1) ANNIE (2) OAKLEY.

"I guess you're right," she said, sitting down. But no sooner did she do that than her head bobbed up expectantly, as if Garry Thunderbird himself might suddenly drop by their table and ask to borrow a pencil. Deanna and Jin-Ha shook their heads.

Admirably, Maggie worked for a full five minutes without stopping.

In minute six:

"So, you guys, who do you think is more fabuloso, Fabio Paolucci or Joel Carlson?"

Deanna looked up from her homework, reluctantly.

"Annie Oakley was probably fabuloso-er than both of them, hands down," she said.

"But between Fabio Paolucci or Joel Carlson, then who?"

"I guess if I had to choose, Joel would be the runner-up. Fabio Paolucci burps in public."

Jin-Ha found herself looking again at the boys clustered around the computer, trying to see what Maggie found so fascinating about them. They still looked the same to her. Why did they all dress exactly alike—blue jacket, untucked T-shirt, jeans, sneakers? In Korea, boys and girls *had* to wear school uniforms and couldn't wait to get to college so they could look *different* from everybody else.

"Joel Carlson looks a little like Garry Thunderbird, don't you think? Around the eyes?" Maggie went on. "He looks sensitive."

Deanna kept working on her homework this time, so Jin-Ha said, "Yeah, I guess so," just to say something, although she found it hard to picture hockey players, who mashed each other with sticks, as sensitive.

"Jin-Ha, you never think any guys are cute," Maggie sighed, a big sigh. "Even Deanna agreed that Joel is fabuloso."

"I never said any such thing," Deanna said huffily. "I said in a field of three, he'd be the number-two runner-up, big deal."

Jin-Ha looked away from the bunch of boys at the computer. It was probably a good thing that she didn't feel what Maggie felt; her parents were traditionally Korean on the subject of dating, and they certainly would forbid her to date at least until she went to college.

6

The next morning, after Jin-Ha dressed for school, she remembered her math homework. The book was still at the bottom of the bag, just where it had been last night.

"Argh," she thought as she tore out a piece of paper from her notebook. She was going to have to copy the answers from the back of the book. It wasn't the right thing to do, but she didn't have any choice. Mr. Arneson gave them a ton of homework every night, but he didn't correct any of it. He just checked to see whether they had done it. She copied down all the answers, erased a couple and wrote them back in to make it look as if she really had done the problems, and shoved the completed paper back in the folder. By then, it was only a few minutes until the bus.

Downstairs, her father was drinking his coffee. He

was in his green jumpsuit with his name, JAY, stitched on the front in heavy yellow thread.

"Did you eat something this morning?" her mother said, worriedly glancing at Jin-Ha's empty place at the table. *"Are you sick?"*

"I'm fine," Jin-Ha said, putting on her coat. *"I'm not that hungry."*

"Don't forget your lunch," her mother said, handing Jin-Ha her lunchbox, which was wrapped in a *pojagi*, a bright cloth used for carrying things.

"Thanks, Mom," Jin-Ha said as she sailed out the door, just in time to catch the big bus rolling up the street.

Deanna was saving her a seat, as she always did. Jin-Ha undid the *pojagi* and took an orange out of her lunch. As she peeled it, little spurts of orange oil sprayed into the air.

"Mmm, like an orange grove," said Deanna, sniffing. "I've said this a million times before, but I love your lunchbox. All the little compartments are so cute."

"Thanks." Jin-Ha offered her friend some orange. In Korea, all the kids had the same kind of flat, rectangular metal lunchbox called a *doshirak*. One big compartment was for rice, the other for *kimchi*, and the two tiny ones were for vegetables, seasoned soybeans, or, on a particular treat day, a boiled egg.

But on the first day here, she had brought her lunchbox to school and everyone had complained about how funny the *kimchi* had smelled. And then Grant Hartwig had grabbed her egg, which she'd just sprinkled with soy sauce, and thrown it around like a baseball.

In America, people didn't carry *doshiraks*. The boys

28

carried their lunches in brown bags, which they threw away. The girls had lunchboxes with colorful pictures of animals or Barbie on the side. Inside would be sandwiches wrapped in waxed paper (sometimes two *different* kinds, maybe one peanut butter, one baloney), wondrously tiny bags of potato chips, juice in a *box*, fruit, and candy. When they were done, the girls threw the wrappers away and closed the box with hooks that snapped smartly like the clasps on a briefcase.

Jin-Ha had begged for a new lunchbox, one with a pony on it. This had surprised her mother.

"This lunchbox is perfectly good, why do you need another?" she had said, as she washed it, along with the utensils, the way she did every night. Jin-Ha couldn't answer. It seemed silly and wasteful on the one hand, but on the other, it would be so wonderful to have a roomy lunchbox that closed like a briefcase and had a picture of a pony on both sides.

"I don't want to eat with chopsticks in front of everyone," she had told her mother. *"With a new lunchbox I could just carry a sandwich."*

Her mother had shaken her head, as if she wasn't recognizing her own daughter. *"If there was something wrong with this, I could see,"* she'd said, holding up the metal case. *"But I don't see any holes in it, do you? Any place where the food might fall out or the rain might come in? Do you see anything?"*

So Jin-Ha had the same old lunchbox, the ghost of Grant Hartwig's mean voice still faintly inside it like the ghost of *kimchi*, which she never carried anymore even though not having it sometimes made her feel like she hadn't eaten lunch at all.

Of course, there were good memories associated with

the lunchbox, too. Of Deanna and Maggie offering to share their cookies with her that first day. Of her mom slipping silly notes—*Sarang hae yo* (I love you)—in with the peanut butter and jelly sandwiches she'd learned to make—and which she cut cleverly to fit into one of the compartments.

"So how's honors math, Miss Brain?" Deanna asked, catching a drip of orange before it fell.

Jin-Ha sighed. When they had gotten their schedules this year, she had noticed an "H" typed next to her math class. Deanna had squealed excitedly and told her that meant she'd been picked for the *honors* math program that went all the way to high school, for the very best math students at Norbuhl Elementary.

"The class is okay," Jin-Ha said. "But I don't know why I'm in it. I'm not that smart in math."

"Yes you are!" said Deanna. "I wish *I* had been picked."

"You're very good in math," said Jin-Ha, and it was true. Jin-Ha had asked her friend for help on more than one occasion. Long division, for instance, had been particularly confusing to her, but to Deanna it had been fun, "like climbing a ladder."

"There are only like two girls in that class, isn't that right?" Deanna asked.

Jin-Ha nodded. "Me and Karen Norgaard. Lori Langstrom was in it, but she dropped out and went to the normal math class."

Lori Langstrom, Jin-Ha remembered, was a very pretty blond girl. She must have been really smart in math because a few times she pointed out mistakes that Mr. Arneson made. Maybe because of that, Mr. Arneson was always teasing her. He would ask her things like, "If you have two pom-poms, and I take away one, what do you have left? A pom?" Or, whenever they had a test, he would say, before he passed it out, "Okay, remember students, no rubbernecking. And Lori," he would add, "no necking." Lori would blush furiously and look angry. After a few weeks, she didn't show up to class anymore, and Mr. Arneson said she had gone back to the "easy" math class because she couldn't handle honors math.

"Lori Langstrom the *cheerleader* was in your class?" Deanna exclaimed. "No way, I'm at least as smart as she is."

"Why didn't you ask the teacher to put you in the class?" Jin-Ha asked her friend. "It would be fun to have you in there, and maybe they didn't know you wanted to be in it."

"I did ask," Deanna admitted. "Mr. Arneson said that our sixth grade math teachers decide who gets into the class, and I guess Mr. Johnson didn't think I was smart enough. You're so lucky. We're still doing fractions and coloring in Venn diagrams. Bo-o-o-ring. Maggie says her class is even slower."

Jin-Ha sighed. If not for math class, she would be breezing through school. American school was so much easier. In Korea, they had school all year with only three weeks off in the summer. And besides that, you had to stay after to clean up your classroom—and then after *that* you went home to extra tutoring or your mountains of homework. There was a saying that if you wanted to get into college, you could only sleep four hours a night—you had so much studying to do. And if you didn't keep up, the teacher could hit your hand with a ruler and make you clean all the toilets. Here, the teachers could only scold you—they couldn't hit you or make you clean the classroom. Even more outrageous, there was a man whose *job* it was to clean up after them.

"Hey there, fabuloso kids!" Maggie was waiting as they got off the bus. Another school day was beginning.

7

In math class, Mr. Arneson collected their homework and then put tomorrow's assignment—twenty problems!—on the board. After that, he started to talk, moving only his mouth and no other parts of his body, not even his eyes, so that he seemed like a Robot Math Teacher, with his speed set on high.

Jin-Ha tried her best to listen, but as usual, she had trouble following Mr. Arneson's thoughts. His words just kept coming and going, one after another and another and another like a row of cars on a train, until she lost track of them. She was relieved when he broke the spell by moving to the blackboard. Jin-Ha copied everything he wrote. When she got home, she promised herself, she'd sit down and figure it all out.

At the end of class, as Jin-Ha was gathering up her books, she saw a NORBUHL BLUEJACKETS HOCKEY jacket hurry out the door.

"Out of the way, four-eyes," Grant Hartwig barked to Karen Norgaard, who had knelt down in the middle of the doorway to tie her shoe.

"Sorry," Karen said. She pushed up her glasses and then skootched over to make room for Grant, who had already pounded past her.

"Stupid jock," she said, waiting until he was out of earshot. She pushed her glasses up again and went on her way.

When Jin-Ha returned home, she found her mother knitting. There was a swatch of material growing on the needles. Jin-Ha loved watching a piece of knitting go from a bunch of tiny yarn loops to a whole sweater you could wrap yourself in. Her mother had shown her how to knit, but Jin-Ha had grown impatient at how slowly the work progressed, and she kept dropping and losing her stitches, which made the piece she was knitting look full of holes.

"How was school?" her mother asked.

"School was fine," Jin-Ha said, and she presented her mother with a test from her science class, a ninety-eight. The big difference between this year and elementary school was that at the end of the marking period they were going to get report cards with real college-type grades—A, B, C, D—on them. That made Jin-Ha feel grown up.

"Very good," her mother said, looking over the test. *"I am lucky to have such a smart daughter. You certainly have a lot of tests, don't you?"*

Jin-Ha nodded. It was true that in Korea, in the lower classes, they didn't really have grades and only a few tests a year. It would catch up to her classmates later when they would have to study incredibly hard for the high

34

school entrance exams and even more important, the college entrance exams. In Korea, only the smartest people could go to college, and Jin-Ha was proud that her parents had *both* gone to *good* colleges. But no wonder her mother was puzzled by the American system. In Korea, teachers would never bother to give seventh graders so many tests, quizzes, weekly spelling tests and so forth.

"How was your day?" Jin-Ha asked.

"I got all the housework done, and dinner, so I had some time to start your father's sweater."

"I see," Jin-Ha said. Sometimes she thought it would be nice if her mother had more friends, people she could just take a walk with or visit. In Korea, she had lots of friends, and Jin-Ha's aunt, *Imo*, and grandma, *Halmoni*, were always coming over. But *Halmoni* and *Imo* were an ocean away.

Someone knocked on their door. Jin-Ha ran to get it. It was Maggie.

"Hey, Maggs," said Jin-Ha. "Come on in."

"Hi," said Maggie. She shook some snow from her shoes and then took them off. Jin-Ha's mother was strict about people removing their shoes before coming in—the way everyone does in Korea—and Jin-Ha appreciated the fact that Maggie never forgot, even though Americans practically wore their shoes to bed!

"Hi, Mrs. Kim," Maggie said.

Jin-Ha's mother smiled. She liked Maggie. "Hello," she said quietly, as she kept knitting.

"Jin, my mom is at the dentist's, and I got sick of reading *Highlights*—aren't Goofus and Gallant just a bunch of dorks?—so I came up here. Is that okay?"

"Of course it's okay," Jin-Ha said. "Does your mom know you're here?"

"Yeah," Maggie said. "She'll come up after she's done—but she might be so puffed up with Novocaine she won't be able to talk."

Jin-Ha's mother put down her knitting. "Hungry?" she asked.

"Um, sorta," said Maggie. "But you don't have to feed me."

"No probl-rem," said Jin-Ha's mother, already disappearing in the kitchen. She reappeared with some rice cakes on a plate.

"Wow, these look fabuloso!" exclaimed Maggie. "What pretty colors: pink, lime green, yellow. Thank you, Mrs. Kim!"

"You welcome," she said, and Jin-Ha smiled at her, so proud her mother was speaking English, she didn't correct her and tell her it was "*you're* welcome."

"These came all the way from Korea," Jin-Ha told Maggie. "Our relatives sent them to us for Christmas. My mom must like you, 'cause she's sharing her secret stash with you."

Maggie popped one in her mouth and chewed. "I love their chewy texture, like gummy bears made out of rice," she declared. "Mrs. Kim, you are fabuloso, like really." Jin-Ha's mother smiled her shy smile, then she took her knitting into the bedroom.

It was nice of her to give them some privacy, Jin-Ha decided. Maggie and Deanna's houses were so huge they almost automatically had privacy, but in this tiny apartment, they were always in someone's way. In Korea, parents would never clear out for a child's guest, but here, her parents were trying to be more accommodating.

"Guess what—I walked with Joel Carlson after school," she told Jin-Ha.

"Really?" Jin-Ha said with some interest. Maggie worked fast. At this rate, she was going to get a boyfriend really soon.

"What'd he say?"

"Say?" Maggie said. "I didn't actually *talk* to him. But when I was leaving school, he was walking out at the same time."

"Oh," Jin-Ha said, a little disappointed.

"But he did look at me," Maggie said. "I swear it. I think it might mean he likes me."

Jin-Ha laughed. She couldn't help it. If Maggie put as much time into studying as she did into thinking about boys, she could be a genius.

Jin-Ha's mother came back into the kitchen and started preparing dinner. Normally, Jin-Ha had to help, but because she had a friend over, Jin-Ha's mother went ahead by herself, putting rice in a pot and swirling water into it.

"Mrs. Kim," Maggie said, wandering into the kitchen. Jin-Ha followed. "There's this guy at school that I like. His name is Joel Carlson. He never really talks to me, but he looks at me. Don't you think that might mean he likes me and maybe he's just shy or something?"

Jin-Ha's mother carefully poured out the milky-looking rice water and put in fresh water, measuring with a finger to make sure the water was at the right level. Then she looked at Maggie and nodded wisely.

"See!" Maggie said triumphantly. "Some guys are just shy."

"Since when did my mom become a dating counselor?" Jin-Ha teased her friend. They both knew Jin-Ha's mother probably only understood about half of what Maggie had said.

The doorbell rang. The two girls ran to get it. It was Mrs. Josephs and Jin-Ha's father, arriving together.

"Hi, Mr. Kim!" shouted Maggie. "Hi, Mom!"

"Hello, Magdalena," Jin-Ha's father replied. Maggie hated being called by her real name, Magdalena ("so long and cumbersome!"), but Jin-Ha's father did it because he knew Mrs. Josephs liked it ("Why give a child such a pretty name if she doesn't use it?").

"How was your appointment, Mom?"

Mrs. Josephs pointed to her jaw, which bulged like a Christmas stocking full of presents.

"Can't talk, huh?" Her mother shook her head. Her hair was a gold color, shiny as tinsel. Jin-Ha knew that Maggie actually got the red in her hair from her mother, who dyed her hair blond.

"You like . . . stay . . . dinner?" asked Jin-Ha's mother. Mrs. Josephs shook her head emphatically no. She was grasping a bottle of Tylenol, and she shook it like it was a pair of maracas.

"Guess I gotta go," Maggie said, putting her coat on. "Thanks again for the rice cakes, Mrs. Kim—they were truly fabuloso!" Jin-Ha's mother smiled at her.

"Bye, Mag-gie," she said. When she called Maggie by her real name, it came out sounding like "Macarena," which would crack Jin-Ha and Maggie up.

8

"We need to go to the super," Jin-Ha's mother declared.

"That's great, I need a walk," Jin-Ha said in English. Another opportunity for her mother to start practicing English, too, she thought.

The two of them put on their jackets. Puffing bravely against the cold, they marched to the WinkyDinky supermarket.

The WinkyDinky was something else. It had no smell and no sound except for some soft, piped-in music. Their market in Korea had smelled like whatever people were selling: spicy rice cakes, fish, or meat. There was always the noise of roosters crowing and merchants calling out about how their merchandise was the best, freshest, and cheapest. The market itself was just plastic tents with the goods in open bins. It wasn't like the WinkyDinky, where the food was wrapped and wrapped again in layers of plastic as if you were just supposed to admire it and weren't ever supposed to open and eat it.

Jin-Ha's mother reviewed the coupons from the Sunday paper, which the Hokanssons gave them when they were finished.

"How's Dad's sweater coming along?" Jin-Ha asked her mother, as she pushed the cart along.

"It's coming," her mother said. *"But I need to work harder on it. I can't knit as fast as I used to."*

"I don't believe that," Jin-Ha said. Her mother knit so fast that her hands blurred and you could practically see things grow before your very eyes. *"You're probably just out of practice."*

"Well, whatever it is, I need to put in more time," she said. *"I want it to be, you know,* fa-bu-lo-so.*"*

"Fabuloso, that's right," Jin-Ha agreed, although she wasn't sure if the word counted as learning English, since Maggie had made it up.

Pushing the cart down the aisle, Jin-Ha marveled, as she always did, at the different cereals: cereals shaped like O's or little pieces of toast or waffles. Cereals with holes or magically woven into little pillows. There was cereal that was supposed to talk to you when you added milk, and cereal that was supposed to be like eating a bowl of cookies. Of course, Jin-Ha would have loved to try some of them, but her mother went right by the vividly colored captains, chocolate vampires, and smiling dinosaurs to the uncooked oats with the white-haired grandfather on the label.

In the "Ethnic Foods" aisle, Jin-Ha's mother pulled a bottle of soy sauce off the shelf and sighed. *"Such tiny bottles! So expensive!"* Back in Korea they used to buy huge tin cans of soy sauce, so big that they seemed to never go dry. Jin-Ha had assumed that in America they could buy Korean food—after all, in Korea you could get American cereal, peanut butter, and even McDonald's. But no, about the only Korean thing they could get at the WinkyDinky was soy sauce, and it wasn't even Korean *kanjang*, it was something called La Choy, which was weak and much sweeter than what they were used to.

A man in a hunting cap looked at them in kind of a funny way as he passed. His head even swiveled as he wheeled his cart by them. There was no doubt he was staring at Jin-Ha and her mother.

Jin-Ha wondered if the man was staring because he heard them speaking Korean. This happened from time to time, and Jin-Ha thought it was very rude. Maybe not a lot of people in Norbuhl spoke Korean, but Deanna's grandma, for instance, spoke Swedish whenever she ran into certain friends and no one stared at *her*.

Jin-Ha was relieved to walk to the meat section, leaving the man in the hunting cap behind.

"Ground beef is on sale," her mother said. Jin-Ha peered into the meat case. There were slabs of red steaks, chicken looking pale and goosepimply. There was also some spicy meat called *porketta* that Italian people ate. CHRISTMAS TURKEYS AND HAMS WILL BE ON SALE DECEMBER 19, a sign said.

"Hm," her mother said, poking the cellophane wrap on a package of ground beef. *"This looks sort of old."*

"Hm," said Jin-Ha, who didn't know the first thing about choosing meat. *"Then let's not get it."*

"No, it's still good to eat, it just looks bad," her mother said. She pulled out her purse and carefully counted her money. *"Maybe we can get a discount on it."*

She put the package of ground beef in Jin-Ha's arms.
"Here, go ask the man if we can get a discount."

Jin-Ha looked at the package of beef she was holding.
It sent a chill up her arms.

*"I don't think you can get a discount in a grocery store
like we do in Korea,"* she told her mother uneasily.
"That's why they have coupons and stuff."

"Just try," her mother urged. The two of them
walked to where one of the butchers was standing in his
soiled apron and stiff white hat.

"Sorry!" her mother said suddenly. "Sorry" was the
word she used to get attention. "Sorry!" she said louder.

The man looked over at her. "Can I help you?" he
asked.

Her mother pointed at Jin-Ha.

The man wiped his hands on his apron.

"You say 'excuse me,' *not* 'sorry,' " Jin-Ha reminded
her mother. The truth was, she didn't want to talk to
this man. He was big, like a bear, and had bristly hairs
growing out of his nose.

"Ask him for a dollar off."

*"Mom, I really don't think you can bargain in a grocery
store,"* Jin-Ha said again.

The butcher, tired of waiting, began to drift away.

"Ask the man," her mother said again.

Jin-Ha didn't know what to do. She raised her hand,
the one with the meat still in it, and said, "Sorry!"

She couldn't believe she'd just said that.

"I mean, excuse me," she said. The man turned
around.

"Yes," he said, hmph-ing a bit now. "What can I *do*
for you?"

"We, uh, well. My mom, um—"

The man looked at her and cocked his head, waiting. *"Go on, ask the man,"* her mother said.

Jin-Ha took a deep breath, then exhaled the question as quickly as possible: "My-mother-wants-to-know-if-you-can-give-her-a-dollar-off-this-ground-beef-because-it-looks-old."

The man looked at them suspiciously, like he thought they were trying to play a trick on him.

"A discount?" the man said. "But it's already on sale."

Jin-Ha didn't know what to do. In Korea, they didn't use pricetags at the market; the price was whatever the seller would give it to you for. If you didn't like one merchant's price, you either asked him to lower it, or you went to the next stall. Jin-Ha had seen her mother do this many times, chatting amiably with half a dozen sellers until they got their groceries at half off. But here in Norbuhl, there was only one grocery store, one place to buy ground beef.

"Show him the spots," Jin-Ha's mother said, pointing to the meat. Her fingers left little dents in the cellophane.

"Mom . . ." Jin-Ha said.

"Just show him the gray spots," her mother said. *"It's not worth four dollars with spots like this."*

Jin-Ha didn't know what to do.

"She says it has gray spots," Jin-Ha told the man.

"Look, kid." The man leaned over. His stiff hat made out of folded paper, tipped with him. "The meat is on *sale*. It's a very *good* price. I don't know what to *tell* you."

"Yes," Jin-Ha said.

"What did he say?" her mother asked. *"Will he cut the price?"*

"No," Jin-Ha said.

"Sorry!" her mother called to the man. He had now gone to the other end of the counter to help, of all people, the man in the hunting cap.

"*Ajushi, kapsun chom kka kka ju sae yo!*" ("*Please, sir, cut the price for us!*") She said this slowly and clearly in Korean, as if that might help the butcher understand her.

The man in the hunting cap turned his potato-shaped nose in their direction and sneered. Then he turned back to the butcher and gave a little smirk. The butcher rolled his eyes just enough that Jin-Ha could see that he was as mean as Hunting Cap.

"Mom," Jin-Ha said, "*maybe we should just not buy meat from here anymore. I don't like that man.*"

Her mother sighed and put the meat back on the pile.

"*The world is strange,*" she said. "*How can it be that there's only one meat seller in this entire town?*"

Jin-Ha sighed, too. At least no one had come out and said anything hurtful, like that time in the bank, but she still worried that it might happen again right here in the WinkyDinky. It was like those tornado watches that showed up at the bottom of their TV screen in the summer. A banner saying something like WARNING! TORNADO WATCH IN EFFECT FROM 5:30 TO 10:00 CENTRAL STANDARD TIME would slowly slide across the screen. A tornado watch, they'd found out, didn't mean there definitely would be a tornado, it just meant that conditions were favorable for them. Some situations were similar; you had to keep alert when the conditions looked threatening.

Jin-Ha and her mother gathered the rest of their groceries and paid without speaking to anyone else. As they were going out, Jin-Ha's eye was caught by a glint of gold. It was Mrs. Josephs, Maggie's mom, coming down the frozen food aisle. They waved to each other and smiled, and Jin-Ha felt a little better.

Jin-Ha's mother made rice with vegetables and little strips of egg for that night's dinner. She had been planning to make "Korean hamburgers"—hamburgers coated in egg, soy sauce, and other spices—but they didn't have any ground beef. Jin-Ha's stomach rumbled after the meal because she hadn't eaten any meat, but she put her hand over it to quiet it down. She didn't want her mother to be more disappointed than she already was over the bargaining.

"*I ate very well,*" her father said, as he got up. He went to the closet and picked up his coat.

"*Time to go,*" he said.

"*Where?*" her mother said, eyebrow raised.

"*My class, of course.*"

"*But I thought your class was on Tuesdays and Thursdays. Today is Wednesday.*"

"*Oh. Today is an extra study session. Sometimes we have them.*"

"*An extra session.*" Jin-Ha's mother rolled down the cuffs of her sleeves. When she cooked, the house warmed up, but it inevitably became cold again, sometimes so cold that she even wore her winter jacket inside the house.

"*They have extra sessions for people who want it. You know me, my English isn't always up to it.*" Jin-Ha's father spoke English very well, of course, but he had told Jin-Ha once that he wanted to learn more "idiomatic expressions." At first, Jin-Ha thought that meant bad words, but he explained that he meant expressions like "she lost

45

her head," which didn't mean literally what the words said. Jin-Ha was also happy to find that both Koreans and Americans said things like "I'm so hungry, I could die!"

"*Your English is very fluent,*" said Jin-Ha's mother.

Jin-Ha's father laughed. "*Thank you for saying so, but I know I need these extra sessions. Perhaps I am too tired from work and don't catch on to everything the first time. It would be nice if I could teach again someday, don't you think?*"

"*Of course,*" Jin-Ha's mother said.

Jin-Ha knew that her mother didn't like it when her father was away, but that she also wanted to help him achieve his dream of becoming a teacher. America was hard on both of them, Jin-Ha was beginning to realize.

"I'll try not to stay out too late," her father said. But Jin-Ha wasn't sure if her mother heard him, since he spoke in English.

9

In math the next day, Mr. Arneson walked around the classroom with a sly smile on his face, like a cat when it's sneaking up on a mouse.

"Put your books under your desks," he said. He was standing in front of them with a sheaf of papers in one hand while sharpening his mustache with the other.

"A test?" said Mike Pakula, the boy sitting in front of Jin-Ha, without even raising his hand. "We don't have a test until next week."

"This isn't a test," Mr. Arneson said. "This is just a little *pop quiz*."

Everyone groaned. Jin-Ha's heart started to thump.

Mr. Arneson nonchalantly licked his fingers and began handing out the test. *Two* sheets. Jin-Ha couldn't understand why he would do such a mean thing.

She stared at the paper in front of her. She had done

all her homework last night, but suddenly, she couldn't remember any of it. "If X and $X1$ are parallel lines cut diagonally by Y . . . "? "If an equilateral triangle had four sides, not three . . ."?

Jin-Ha looked out the window. It had been clear this morning, but now the sky stretched out gray as far as the eye could see, and snow was gently wafting down. How she would like to be outside trying to catch the feathery snowflakes on her tongue. She tore her eyes away from the window and forced herself to look only at the test.

"If the sides of a triangle are X, $X+1$, and $X+2$ . . ." She skipped to the third problem.

"Time's up," Mr. Arneson said. Jin-Ha looked at him in disbelief. She had barely begun the problems on the second page.

"We have a lot to go over today, so hand them in quick."

Everyone turned in their papers with the usual moans and groans. Jin-Ha looked across the aisle at Karen Norgaard to see how she had weathered the test, but the light bounced off Karen's big glasses, hiding her eyes. Grant Hartwig put his books back on his desk with an intentionally loud thump and looked bored. Jin-Ha tried to tell herself that this was just a quiz, a little surprise quiz that couldn't be worth too much, but she wanted to bury her head in her arms and howl.

After school, Maggie, Deanna, and Jin-Ha went to Maggie's house. Jin-Ha almost didn't go. She was still feeling queasy from her math test, but Maggie and Deanna convinced her she needed a snack.

"Here," said Maggie, bringing out a tray of different kinds of cookies and big glasses of milk. "These aren't as fabuloso as the ones we had at your house, Jin, but they'll have to do."

Jin-Ha took a Christmas cookie from the tray. Her hunger was returning. She especially loved cookies with colored sugar sprinkles, which she would scrape off with her teeth before eating the cookie itself. Deanna took a gingerbread man and bit off his head. Maggie skipped the Christmas cookies for three Oreos, which she carefully unscrewed and laid out in front of her as if she were playing solitaire.

"Look," she said. "Six cookies in place of three, and the same amount of calories."

Deanna laughed. "What is this, the new Maggie math?"

"Actually," Maggie said, "my mother said now that I turned twelve, I have to start watching what I eat."

"Why?" asked Jin-Ha. She tried to imagine Maggie's food trying to run away from her while she wasn't looking.

"Because otherwise I'll get fat and then I'll never get a date. Boys hate fat girls. I might even go on this diet where you eat a lot of pineapple and Jell-O but you can't have *any* cookies."

Oh, *watch what you eat*. Be mindful of calories and all that. An idiomatic expression.

"Oh, Maggie," Jin-Ha said, laughing. "I thought you meant you had to watch your food."

"Well, the notorious Jimmie the Twerp has been known to steal the food off her plate if they're having something good," Deanna said. "But right now she's talking about dieting."

"But if you don't eat enough, you won't grow or you might get sick," Jin-Ha said worriedly.

"That's true," Deanna agreed, biting the head off another gingerbread man. "Tell your mom that guys don't like sickly dwarf girls, either."

Maggie pushed her lip out in a pout. "Are you saying my mom is wrong or weird or something?"

Jin-Ha stopped short. She tried to think of the situation from Maggie's point of view. "I'm sorry, Maggie," she said. "Deanna and I weren't making fun of your mom. We were just worried about your health."

"Yeah," Deanna added. "You're a stick right now. Why don't you wait until you look like Russell Zamboni? *He* needs to go on the pineapple and Jell-O diet!" Russell Zagoni was this very large guy who'd graduated from high school two years ago. When he walked around town, his fat jiggled around him as if it had a life of its own. People called him Russell Zamboni because he was as big as a Zamboni, the truck that smooths the ice before hockey games. But Russell was very, very good-natured about his weight and just laughed along with the people who made the jokes. Like Santa, Jin-Ha supposed.

Maggie smiled a little, then grabbed another Oreo and ate it after dunking the whole thing in her milk, which bubbled over the side a bit. Jin-Ha smiled back at her. The house was very warm, heated by the big rumbly furnace in the basement.

"So what's everyone getting their families for Christmas?" Deanna asked.

"I'm think I'm buying my mom a new blowdryer," Maggie said. "The kind with the magic fingers that make your hair fuller. For my dad I'm getting some Miner

Man cologne, and Jeri is getting earrings. For Jimmie the Twerp, I have this feeling that Santa might be bringing him a lump of coal because he's been horrible all year. Just yesterday, he pulled Playdough's tail *twice*."

"Hm, those are excellent ideas," Deanna said. "Except for the lump of coal."

Exchanging gifts at Christmas was new to Jin-Ha and her parents. In Korea, you either paid a lot of attention to Christmas or you didn't at all. Her family had been the kind who didn't pay attention because they were Buddhist, not Christian. Here in the U.S., though, it seemed like everyone got into Christmas whether they were Christian or not—they even had a Christmas pageant in school! Jin-Ha admittedly liked the songs, and the story of the Baby Jesus lying in a manger surrounded by gentle animals. And she liked how people got ready for Christmas starting in November, preparing and thinking about special gifts to give. It was something to look forward to during the whole dark month of December.

Last year, Jin-Ha and her parents had prayed together on Christmas Eve, and on Christmas morning her father had opened up a box that held three green mugs. The Hokanssons had given them some spicy-smelling Christmas tea, and all three of them had drunk out of their new mugs. It wasn't exchanging gifts exactly, but her parents said thinking about things other members of the family might need was a nice custom.

Jin-Ha knew that Deanna and Maggie's families bought special gifts for *everyone* that they wrapped in special Christmas paper and put under a tree that they actually brought from the forest into the house. Of course, Deanna and Maggie had money to buy presents because they babysat. Jin-Ha's parents wouldn't let her do that—they said she needed to spend all her time studying.

This year Jin-Ha wanted to give gifts, real gifts that were wrapped and kept a secret until Christmas morning. Her father was already getting that sweater, so why not get something for her mother? Gift giving was fun no matter what your religion.

"Ugh, I haven't even gone shopping yet," said Deanna. "How about you, Jin?"

"I haven't gone shopping yet, either."

"Maybe we should just wait for the after-Christmas sales." Deanna sighed. "I never know what to get for anybody."

"Me, too," Jin-Ha said.

10

Mr. Arneson didn't return their quizzes that week, which wasn't all that strange, because he tended to be very slow. Other teachers corrected and gave you back the test the next day. Jin-Ha wondered what Mr. Arneson did with his time, since he was done every day at three in the afternoon, while other people, like her father, worked well into the evening. But she didn't really mind about the test—no news is good news, as they said. Perhaps on the way home from school a huge gust of wind had blown them out of his hands and into a sewer. You never know.

But soon the week of their real test rolled around, and they still hadn't gotten their quizzes back. A few kids grumbled, and Mr. Arneson promised he'd get them back soon.

The night before their math test, Jin-Ha sat down early to study. She had an uneasy feeling about the things they'd been learning lately—Mr. Arneson's lectures barely made sense to her, and she turned to the back to see the homework answers much more than she ever used to.

She stared at her math book. It hadn't magically begun to make sense with the passing of the hour, the way she hoped it would. She was very, very tired. It got dark early these days, and the heaviness of it seemed to be pressing on her eyelids.

Black Beauty stared at her. Maybe before she really got down to studying, she could read for a few minutes to get her blood going. Just the first paragraph or so . . .

*

"Good luck on your math test," Jin-Ha's mother said, spooning a little more oatmeal into her bowl. *"Eat a lot so you'll have lots of energy."*

Jin-Ha didn't feel like eating: the Mr. Quaker oatmeal was about as appealing as a mound of wet concrete. How had she fallen asleep like that? It seemed as if one minute she was reading her book and the next she had woken up with her head on her desk, crushing the pages of *Black Beauty*. In a panic she had attacked her math book, but within minutes, her dreams had slithered back, beckoning enticingly just behind her eyelids. It was two in the morning, and her eyelids felt like window shades that someone was trying very hard to pull shut.

In the end, she had given up and crawled to bed, telling herself she'd get up early and study—you couldn't study when you couldn't stay awake, right? But she had somehow slept through her alarm, and now she was late.

"Here," her mother said. She rolled a few walnuts toward Jin-Ha.

"What's this for?" Jin-Ha said.

"For brain power," her mother said, picking up one of the nuts. *"It's good for your brain. See how it looks just like a brain, with all the wrinkles and crevices?"*

"So eating walnuts will help my brain?" Jin-Ha said, starting to smile a little, despite herself.

"I'm sure of it," said her mother. *"I'll crack a few and put them in your lunch."*

Jin-Ha studied as best she could while waiting for the bus and on the ride to school. Deanna obligingly didn't talk to her, and Jin-Ha passed her some of the walnuts she was nibbling on. Between classes, Jin-Ha got in a few more minutes of studying, and she felt much better.

In math class, Mr. Arneson had the cat-smile on his face again.

"First, let me pass out the quiz, so you can get a better idea of where you stand," he said.

Everyone groaned.

He passed back everyone's quiz, face down. Jin-Ha wasn't sure if she should look, but everyone else was. She grasped the corner of it and lifted. All she saw at first was two parallel lines . . . connected by another line.

An F.

An F??

A one-legged A, was what her science teacher Mr. Feron called them. That was funny. But not when the F was happening to her.

"Take a second and look the quiz over." She barely heard Mr. Arneson's voice; it sounded far away, like her grandmother's voice on the phone from Korea.

Mr. Arneson licked his fingers and began to pass out the test. When Mike Pakula, who sat in front of her, handed her the pile of tests, Jin-Ha just sat there in shock. She couldn't move, couldn't breathe. An F! What was she going to do?

"C'mon, hurry up!" said Mike, wiggling the tests at her as if Jin-Ha couldn't see them.

Jin-Ha reluctantly took the pile. She smoothed her test on her desk and wrote her name on the corner. Actually, it didn't look *that* hard. She did problems one, two, three, and four.

But page two was *all* story problems. One of them was about a boy, Johnny, who was trying to buy a bunch of things with a certain number of nickels, dimes, and quarters. As Jin-Ha tried to figure it out, she couldn't help thinking, now, who would want to do that, anyway? To pay for something with a whole pile of change was rude. Math was so useless.

Jin-Ha realized she was sweating in the cool classroom. Even the problems that had looked easy seemed suddenly hard.

When Mr. Arneson asked for the tests, she handed hers in. At least she had filled in more answers than she had on the quiz. Jin-Ha saw Karen hand in her test with a little cat-smile of her own.

"What did you think of the test?" Jin-Ha couldn't help asking her. Karen shrugged and twirled a lank bit of blond hair the exact same way Mr. Arneson twirled his mustache.

"It was okay," she said. She stopped playing with her hair. "It was lots easier than the quiz."

"I thought so, too," Jin-Ha said, a little reassured. At

the very least, she had done better on this one, and a test was worth much more than a quiz.

When Jin-Ha got home, she found her mother finishing up a batch of vegetable tempura, laying it on paper towels to drain. She had cut up carrots, sweet potatoes, and onions and made some homemade batter. Once the veggies were fried, they were so pretty they looked like toys. As was her custom, she had already set some aside on a plate to be taken to the Hokanssons.

The Hokanssons were nice neighbors. They gave the Kims their Sunday paper when they were through with it, complete with coupons! And when Jin-Ha's father had a question about the way things worked in the apartment, Mr. Hokansson was always there to lend a hand.

Once, they had had the Hokanssons over for dinner. Jin-Ha's mother hadn't known how to make American food then, so she had served *kimchi*, rice, and tempura. Jin-Ha didn't think Mr. and Mrs. Hokansson were too crazy about the spicy *kimchi*, but they had seemed to like the tempura. Mrs. Hokansson said the onion pieces reminded her of onion rings—her favorite food—so whenever Jin-Ha's mother made tempura, she always fried up a few extra pieces for the Hokanssons.

"*Mom*," Jin-Ha said, picking up the plate and holding it out to her mother, "*why don't you bring these over for a change? After all, you did all the work.*"

Jin-Ha's mother didn't make a move to take the plate. "*Maybe some other time,*" she said gently. "*Now hurry before they get cold.*"

Jin-Ha took the plate and went out into the hall. Mr. Hokansson opened the door. He had the evening paper in his hands and was wearing slippers.

"Well hello, there," he said to Jin-Ha. "If it isn't our little neighbor girl."

"Hi, Mr. Hokansson," Jin-Ha said, holding out the plate of tempura. "My mother made you and Mrs. Hokansson some tempura."

"Now, isn't that thoughtful!" Mr. Hokansson said. "Margie will be pleased to bits—she likes those onion rings, you know."

"I know," Jin-Ha said. She wondered what Mrs. Hokansson did all day. Both of the Hokanssons were retired, although Jin-Ha knew Mr. Hokansson did a lot of volunteer work at the library because she saw him there, re-shelving books, all the time.

"Well, thanks so much, Jin-Ha," Mr. Hokansson said. "I do believe Margie is defrosting some of our summer rhubarb, so you just might get you some rhubarb bars on the plate when it's returned."

"Oh, yum!" said Jin-Ha. She loved Mrs. Hokansson's sour-sweet rhubarb bars. "Oh," she said, suddenly inspired. "Maybe someday Mrs. Hokansson can teach my mother how to make them."

The phone rang inside the apartment.

"Sorry, got to go," Mr. Hokansson said. Jin-Ha reluctantly said goodbye. She hoped Mr. Hokansson had heard her last sentence.

When Jin-Ha went back to the apartment, she made sure to mention to her mother that they might get some rhubarb bars—and a visitor—soon. Maybe *that* would get her to start practicing her English, who knows?

11

The next week, Mr. Arneson handed the tests back. Jin-Ha turned hers over.

There was a "plus"—but with an F attached to it.

She couldn't believe it! She felt like someone had just punched her in the face—and then landed another punch in her stomach.

She stole a look at Karen. Maybe everyone in the class had gotten a bad grade.

B-plus. "Good job". When Karen saw her looking, she frowned and covered her test with her arm.

Jin-Ha didn't know what to do. This was the first time in her life that she had ever done this badly in school. A B or a C was one thing, but an F? How had this happened? How would she get into college now?

*

"You've been quiet like a mouse today," Deanna remarked, as they rode the bus home.

"Huh?" Jin-Ha said.

Deanna laughed. "Can you hear me? Can you see me?" She waved her hands in front of Jin-Ha's eyes, the way a hypnotist might to make sure a patient was in a trance.

"Oh, sorry," Jin-Ha said. "I'm just tired."

Jin-Ha walked into the apartment. She didn't see her mother, but from the kitchen she heard the familiar whoosh-whoosh sounds of rice being washed.

"Jin-Ha? How was school?" her mother asked.

"Fine," Jin-Ha said.

"Are you hungry? Want some kimchi?"

"No thanks," Jin-Ha said. She held her breath, then started to tiptoe to her room.

"Did you get your math test back yet?" Her mother had been asking her this every day. Sometimes Jin-Ha wished she didn't keep such meticulous track of things. She was glad her mother couldn't see her face.

"We did."

"How did you do?"

"Fine."

"What kind of grade did you get?"

Jin-Ha gulped. Her mother had never known her to get such an awful grade. How could she explain that she was still studying hard but had gotten terrible grades? Her parents always said that a bad outcome in school was merely the result of laziness. Her mother's favorite expression was, "Any tree will fall if you chop at it long and hard enough." But maybe her mother would understand that in America, things were different: just as she couldn't learn English fast enough, Jin-Ha couldn't learn math fast enough, either.

"I got an F-plus," Jin-Ha admitted in a small voice.

"An F?" her mother said. *"What kind of grade is that?"*

Jin-Ha suddenly realized that her mother didn't know about American grades: they didn't have A, B, C, D—and F—in the Korean language. She had only known about number grades up until now.

"F is for . . ." her brain whirred like a pinwheel in the wind.

Her mother smiled. She looked so proud. She was of course expecting to hear that F was a good grade.

Jin-Ha opened her mouth.

"F is for . . . fabuloso!" is what came out.

It was like someone else had said it, not her, like the time she had accidentally said a bad word. The word had floated in the air and stayed there, like the balloon words of a comic book character. Now, again, her words were practically visible in front of her face: F IS FOR FABULOSO!!! F IS FOR FABULOSO! Too late to call them back.

"Fabuloso," her mother smiled. *"That is so wonderful. An F-plus! I think that calls for an extra treat for dinner, my studious daughter."*

Jin-Ha gulped. How to fix this? She had never lied to her mother before. She hadn't meant to this time, either. She just wanted her mother to be happy, that's all. Was a lie really a lie when you didn't mean it to be?

When her father came home, Jin-Ha's mother excitedly told him about the wonderful job Jin-Ha was doing in her math class. At least, Jin-Ha thought, her father would know what an F was, since he went to school here. Once he asked what grade she got, the whole misunderstanding would be revealed.

"Now," said her father, smiling broadly, "aren't you glad you took that math class? You thought it would be too hard for you."

Why hadn't he asked her what her grade was?

"Um, I'm not doing *that* well," she started.

"Don't underestimate yourself," her father said. "I can see how hard you study, and you see, it's paying off. As your mother and I are always saying, education is the most important thing in life. Once you have good grades, no one can take that away from you. And without good grades, you won't get very far in life."

Jin-Ha's heart was sinking, lower and lower. She wanted to yell, "I got an F!" but the words wouldn't come out, even though she opened her mouth to say them. She felt oddly paralyzed, as if she were waiting for some fourth person to come out of the walls and explain everything for her.

She was the only person who could say something. But as long as she didn't say a word, her parents would stay happy. She liked seeing them that way: her father beaming, her mother bustling happily about the kitchen. It would ruin everything to tell them that F was for failure.

She waited to see what would happen next. Maybe her parents would see that she wasn't all excited, too. Maybe her father would come out and ask her, "You didn't get an F, did you?" If they did something like that, it would give her an opening in which to slip in the bad news.

Her parents just smiled at her.

"I have a lot of homework to do," Jin-Ha told her parents.

"By all means, get to work," her father said, humming under his breath. "I'll help your mother with dinner."

Jin-Ha went upstairs to her room. She took out her two F tests, and instead of putting them in her desk drawer, where she normally kept her tests, she stuck them deep into the pages of her math book where nobody would ever see them. Then she put a pillow over her head and wished that this day would just disappear, totally.

12

Jin-Ha dreamed there were a bunch of *X*'s chasing her. Mr. Arneson was there—first he was very small, like a spider, but then he grew large and spoke in a voice that was so loud that the trees in their classroom shivered and shook.

The rattling of her window woke her up. Jin-Ha's nose felt like a cold metal thimble in the middle of her face, and her left hand, which had fallen out of the covers during the night, was uncomfortably chilly as well. The rest of her, at least, was warm under the thick covers. The clock, shining brightly in the cold air of her room, declared it to be 6:55. The sky had not yet begun to lighten, and by the light of the streetlamp, Jin-Ha could see hard fingers of frost pressing on her window. She wanted to stay in her warm bed and never come out. Being cold—and knowing you were going to be even colder before you got any warmer—was the worst feeling.

Then she remembered her dream.

Then she remembered the math test.

Now she wanted to jump out of bed and onto the first bus out of town.

How else to cope with this terrible thing she had done? She had failed two math tests *and* she had lied to her parents. Lying to her parents had been ten times worse than telling them the truth: Telling the truth would have gotten the unpleasant news over with right away. By lying, she was only postponing the agony. Everything only *seemed* all right; underneath, it was all wrong. ALL WRONG.

But running away wouldn't work, either. At least not now. She didn't have a suitcase big enough to pack all the winter clothes she would need.

Jin-Ha reluctantly got up, danced around in the cold, and got ready for school.

"I'm in trouble," Jin-Ha told Deanna on the bus.

Deanna leaned forward in the seat. "You? In trouble for what?"

She told Deanna what happened. On her way out this morning, her mother had called *"Keep up the good work,"* so she was still fooled.

"Wow, Jin-Ha," she said. "That *is* bad."

"I want to run away."

"Don't run away—you'll freeze and we won't find you until spring," Deanna said, patting her arm. "It's not *that* bad. We'll figure something out."

"Not only have I never gotten such a bad grade, I've never lied to my parents before, either," Jin-Ha said miserably. She didn't understand how she'd gotten herself into this mess! She always thought of herself as a good kid who didn't give her parents any trouble, not like the naughty blue frogs in the Korean folktale who did the opposite of everything their parents told them to do and only later came to regret their actions.

"Hey, look." Maggie pointed to a poster on the wall as soon as she saw Jin-Ha and Deanna. "The theme of the Christmas dance is going to be 'Ice Castles.' Isn't that romantic?"

"Maggie, can you stop thinking about boys for like two seconds?" Deanna said.

"It's Magdalena—please."

"I thought you hated being called that."

"I changed my mind. Maggie sounds so plain, like someone's Irish setter puppy or something. Magdalena is mysterious and womanly."

Deanna sighed. "Whatever. We have to help Jin-Ha out."

"Help her what?"

Jin-Ha told Maggie what happened.

"So what's the problem?" Maggie said. "Just tell your parents what F really means: fail. It's just one test and a quiz, no big poops."

"But everything's so weird now," Jin-Ha said, alarmed. "It's not just the F, it's the fact I lied."

"Your parents are so nice," Maggie said. "I'm sure they'll understand."

"They are nice," Jin-Ha said. "But grades are really important to them, and they are going to be furious when they find out I lied to them."

Maggie crunched up her face.

"I don't know then," she said. "Maybe you should

move away and start a new life with a new identity—I saw that on a TV show."

"Maggie—be serious!" said Deanna.

"It's Magdalena, please," Maggie said. "And I don't know what to do. I really don't. If Jin-Ha doesn't want to tell them the truth, well, she's going to have to learn to live with her lie. I can't tell her what to do."

The trouble was, Jin-Ha didn't know what to do, either.

13

In homeroom, Jin-Ha received a note that she was supposed to go see Mr. Arneson. Her heart sank. She took the pink pass and trudged over to her math classroom.

"Please sit down, Gina," he said, when she arrived. Jin-Ha hated it when people called her "Gina." Her name was clearly spelled Jin–hyphen–Ha. But half the time when she got up the courage to correct people, they looked at her like she didn't know her own name! She *knew* she had corrected Mr. Arneson more than once, and she seemed to recall he'd even spent a few seconds practicing, huffing, "Jin-Ha, Jin-Ha." But it must not have done him any good.

"I'm sure you know why I called you in," he said. His voice seemed to bounce around the empty classroom.

"Because of my bad math grades?"

He nodded and shuffled some papers around on his desk. "You know you can do much better than that," he said. He had taken off his glasses, and his eyebrows were a single furry caterpillar lying lazily across his forehead.

"It seems strange for your grades to drop so suddenly," he said. "You were getting A-minus/B-plus up till now. Are you having problems at home?"

"Oh, no," Jin-Ha said.

Mr. Arneson sighed. "Mr. Johnson, your sixth grade math teacher, said you were an excellent student."

Jin-Ha didn't remember anything about sixth grade math except that it hadn't given her all the trouble this math class was giving her.

"So you can certainly handle the work," Mr. Arneson went on. "And there's no excuse for those lousy test scores. In fact, no one in honors math should flunk a test, in my humble opinion."

Jin-Ha didn't know what to say. She didn't want to tell him that he seemed to be speaking a foreign language when he taught and that his thoughts seemed to ricochet all over the place. She didn't want to tell him that this was the only class where she felt like that.

"Do you think maybe," Jin-Ha said, shifting in her seat, "that I can get a little extra help from you—after school, or during lunch?"

"Help?" said Mr. Arneson. "All the help you need is right in the book. In class I tell you kids everything you need to know, and then you've got the book and the homework. It all runs together. What would you need extra help for?"

"But you don't correct the homework," Jin-Ha said. She could hear her voice growing more and more timid.

69

She didn't like it when that happened. She tried clearing her throat. Be brave, like Shim Cheong the bravest girl in the world, she reminded herself.

Mr. Arneson leaned back and sighed a big, mournful sigh, as if Jin-Ha was the most troublesome student he'd ever encountered.

"The answers are in the back of the book, you know," he said.

"I know," Jin-Ha said, her voice starting strong, but starting to fade again. "But sometimes when I get things wrong, I don't understand why."

"Why? Why, you just need to study harder," he said, as if the answer were written in front of her, in big letters. "You can't expect me to give you special treatment, now, can you? Do you think that would be fair to the others?" He stared hard at Jin-Ha. She could hear his breath flowing through his nose. It was like a dragon breathing.

"I guess not," Jin-Ha said, after a minute. What else could she say? "I'll try to study harder."

"That's what I like to hear," Mr. Arneson boomed. "Besides, you people are the ones who are supposed to be naturals at math."

Jin-Ha stared at her teacher. Who was "you people"? Did he know that her mother was good in math? Did he mean girls?

"We're scheduled to have three, maybe four tests from now until the end of the term." Mr. Arneson opened up his grade book and frowned. "So you do have plenty of chances to redeem yourself—all you have to do is apply yourself a bit."

Those tests were her last chance. If she did well

enough to recover her A-minus, her parents would never know about the F's. But could she study hard enough on her own to do that?

She remembered her mother, and how proud and happy she was the night she was fooled into believing an F was a good grade. And her father, even though he was exhausted from work, had smiled a huge smile because he believed Jin-Ha was doing well in school.

"I'll study!" Jin-Ha said, now almost shouting.

"That's the spirit," Mr. Arneson said, smiling broadly.

That night, before she went off to the library with her friends, Jin-Ha sat up in her room and looked over her tests. It was like another story problem: If Jin-Ha has taken five tests and three quizzes that average ninety, and then she does terribly on one quiz and a test, what scores does she have to get on the next three tests and X quizzes in order to bring her grade back up?

Mr. Kim walked Jin-Ha, Deanna, and Maggie to the library after dinner. Mrs. Josephs would pick all three girls up at nine-thirty

"Study hard," Jin-Ha's father said to her. There was real pride in his voice, and Jin-Ha felt awful.

"Ah, just in time," said Maggie, as they entered the warm building. "My ears feel ready to break off." They looked brittle, like tiny pink shells.

"Then try wearing a hat," Deanna advised, as she pulled off her thick wool cap. Charged with static electricity, her hair levitated all over the place.

"Nuh uh," said Maggie, cupping her hands over her

ears. "I don't want to get hat-head. You look like a dan-delion before you blow on it."

"And *you're* going to look like Vincent Van Gogh," Deanna countered. They giggled.

Jin-Ha made her way to the book return bin; it was time to return *Black Beauty* and all her bee books. She dug in her book bag. Her math book was on top for a change. She grabbed it and the books she meant to re-turn. As always, she felt a little sad to be giving up her books, thinking that before she checked them out again, some other kid might borrow them, maybe get food on their pages.

Jin-Ha strained to lift the books to fit into the narrow slot on top of the tall bin, but in a terrible coincidence, someone else started putting books in from the other side.

Jin-Ha's books missed the slot and tumbled to the floor, as did the other person's. She looked up.

The other person was Grant Hartwig. Mean Grant Hartwig.

The remaining books in her hand slid and crashed to the floor.

"Here, I'll get them," he said. "I should have looked before I dumped my books in—sorry."

Jin-Ha was dumbfounded. Grant Hartwig knew words like "sorry"? She stood, puzzled, as Grant bent his tall body down to the floor, gathered up her books, and stacked them in her arms like firewood. Then he picked up his own.

At that moment, Maggie walked by. Her eyes opened wide when she saw Jin-Ha and Grant Hartwig together. Jin-Ha found herself blushing. To avoid looking at either

Maggie or Grant, she started putting her books into the return bin, one at a time. When she was done, Grant put his in.

"Well, see you," he said.

"OhmyGod, ohmyGod, I saw you talking with Grant Hartwig!" Maggie said in a strangled whisper as soon as Jin-Ha sat down at their table. "What did he say?"

"Nothing. We weren't really talking."

"Maggie," said Deanna, "Grant Hartwig is that evil boy who called Jin-Ha a 'chink,' like the first day poor Jin-Ha got here. And don't forget that time he stole her egg."

"But he's a hockey player," breathed Maggie.

"My point exactly," said Deanna.

"So what were you talking about?" Maggie demanded.

"Nothing, as I said. We bumped books trying to return them." Jin-Ha was still confused, wondering how the boy who said "Sorry" and retrieved her books could be the same boy who called her names.

"In this book I just bought, *How to Talk to Boys*," Maggie said excitedly, "it said you should have stuff ready to talk about, like sports or hunting and fishing. It said if you follow their rules, you will *definitely* get a date in thirty days."

"Maggie, I'd *love* to hear what *you* have to say about hunting and fishing!" Deanna laughed. "That one time we all went fishing you wouldn't touch a worm."

"It's Magdalena—how many times do I have to tell you?" Maggie said, then she sniffed. "Just because I don't like worms doesn't mean I don't have anything to say about fishing."

Deanna rolled her eyes. She knew that Maggie loved animals and couldn't hurt a fly.

"Let's study," Jin-Ha said. "Or else the librarian will get mad."

"No kidding, Maggs," said Deanna. "Try to get your report in on time for a change!"

Maggie grumbled, but, perhaps remembering how she had handed her Annie Oakley report in late—and for half a grade lower—she ducked her head and began to read.

Jin-Ha turned to her math homework. She looked at her notes, then at the book. They had gone over almost a whole chapter today and she was lost. But where could she go for help? Could she possibly get Mr. Arneson to slow down? He didn't seem like a very sympathetic man.

She sighed. Wouldn't it be nice if they would just let you concentrate on what you were good at in school? She liked to read, and she liked science. Maybe if she got fantastic grades in science and English, her parents wouldn't care what she got in math. After all, she knew how to add and subtract and multiply and divide—the important grocery-store stuff.

Fat chance. How could she handle going to college if she failed junior high math?

She sighed again and turned to the back of her book to peek at the answers. They were already neatly checked off in pencil. Jin-Ha never wrote in her books. She flipped open the cover. A few papers tumbled out and revealed, in neat, squarish handwriting, GRANT O. HARTWIG. She looked into her bag. Her math book wasn't there. Grant must have picked his own book off the floor and accidentally given it to her and vice versa.

Jin-Ha picked up the tests and homeworks that had fallen out and put them back in the book. But she couldn't help noticing that his tests were all A's—not even A-minuses—including the test and quiz she had failed. Jin-Ha was curious now: The boy who seemed so awful was pretty smart at math, wasn't he? She picked up the last test. Grant's writing was neat and ordered, as if he already knew the answers before working out the problem. No scratch-outs, no erasures done so many times they wore a hole in the paper like Jin-Ha's tests.

She turned to the problem with Johnny's nickels, dimes, and quarters. She had used hash marks to try to figure out the number of coins he needed. Grant had just written everything out neatly into an equation: $.05x + .10(2x-x) + .25(3x) = \$2.70$.

And of course he had the right answer:

nickels = 3
dimes = 3 (6–3)
quarters = 9

This test almost seemed magical, so neat and clean, Jin-Ha thought.

She decided she should give Grant his book back.

"Where are you going?" Maggie asked her.

"This isn't my book, it's Grant Hartwig's," she said. "I'm going to return it and get mine back."

Jin-Ha found the hockey players clustered around the computer, as usual. They were playing some game that involved a lot of shooting. Grant looked up when he saw her with the book in her hand.

"I have your math book," she said.

He looked confused.

"Our books must have gotten switched at the return bin," Jin-Ha went on. "You must have mine."

"Fartwig has a girlfriend," one of the boys said, turning his attention from the screen to her. Jin-Ha gulped.

"Give me that, you friggin' jap math geek," Grant said, grabbing the book back and shoving into his bag. He fumbled in his hockey bag for her book and then he let it fall to the floor. The papers inside it slipped out all over the place.

Jin-Ha went to pick up her book, but one of the other hockey players deftly scooped it up first. He held it out to her, but just as Jin-Ha's fingers were about to touch it, he jerked it away.

"Chinky-chinky wanna wanna bookee?" he said, sneering at her.

Jin-Ha grabbed for her book again. This time she was sure she had it, but the boy tossed it to his friend who made buck teeth at her and said, "Ah-so, Confucius say vely nice bookee, you want?"

Jin-Ha felt tears stinging her eyes. How could these boys be so mean?

"Boys!" Miss Rungewiler, the librarian, had come to survey the scene. Jin-Ha liked her very much, and she was relieved to see her.

"What is going on here?" she asked Jin-Ha.

Jin-Ha blinked away her tears, steadied her voice.

"Those boys have my math book."

"Give it back to her," Miss Rungewiler said sternly. The boy handed it over to her.

"Now, you boys better quit fooling around or you'll

be asked to leave. This is a *public* library, you know. You have ten minutes left on that computer."

When she went back to the desk, a couple of the boys made fun of Miss Rungewiler's limping walk. One of them mumbled, "You old witch," under his breath. Now that she had the book, Jin-Ha knew she'd better get out of there.

Then she remembered the tests.

They were strewn out on the floor, her F tests lying face-up for everyone to see.

She snatched up the papers and her book and ran back to the other side of the library, where her friends were.

"So what happened? What happened?" said Maggie excitedly, when she saw Jin-Ha return.

"Nothing, Maggie," Jin-Ha sighed. Her face was on fire, and she thought she might start crying. What was wrong with those boys? She felt tears rise in her eyes but she pushed them down. Why trouble her friends? She didn't want Maggie to be late with her report this time.

"Hey, are you okay?" Maggie said, concerned. "Your face is all red."

"It's hot in here," Jin-Ha said. At least that was true. She opened her math book and pretended to read it.

"Did Grant say anything to you?" Maggie wanted to know.

Jin-Ha pretended she was deep into her math, and barely shook her head.

"C'mon, Maggie," Deanna said. "We all know hockey players are dorks with no manners. We only have an hour to go—forget boys, let's study."

Jin-Ha was relieved that her friends hadn't seen or

heard what happened with the boys. She settled back into doing her math homework, but now it was impossible to concentrate. How bad Grant Hartwig was! She had just been trying to be nice, and he'd called her names—again!

"I'm going to go out and get some air," Jin-Ha said suddenly, grabbing her coat.

"Are you okay?" Maggie asked again.

"I'm fine," Jin-Ha said. "I just need some air to clear my head. It's stuffy in here."

"Do you want one of us to come out with you and keep you company?" asked Deanna.

"No, I'll be fine," Jin-Ha said.

She stepped out in front of the library. The light from the library made everything outside look even darker. She felt dark herself. She was lost in math and tangled up in an awful lie, *and* all the hockey players were picking on her. She suddenly wished she was in Korea again with Kyung-Hee and Ji-Sun. Over there, things didn't seem as hard as they were here. Everyone was Korean and did things the Korean way. They would all be at the Plum Flower school together, and after school they would play jacks and eat snacks from the market without anyone bothering them.

Tears began falling. She sniffed, desperate to stop them, but they tracked icily down her face, two tears becoming four, then six and eight. Oh, what am I going to do? she thought miserably. She couldn't go back into the library *crying*, now could she?

*   *   *

The library door swung open, and Jin-Ha saw the hockey players clambering out in one blue crowd. She ducked her head and tried to tuck herself deeper into her coat. It was tornado watch time. *I'm not here, you don't notice me, I'm not here,* she repeated in her head over and over.

It worked. They didn't notice her. Someone was telling a joke about something, and they all laughed. In one noisy mass, they disappeared down the street, their shouts and hoots swallowed up quickly by the frigid air. Jin-Ha breathed a sigh of relief, a pure white cloud. It was freezing outside, but she was beginning to like it, even the way her tears were stuck to her face in icy beads.

A few minutes later, a figure approached in the dark. Who could it be? The library would be closing in an hour. The person looked like an adult, but as the shape came closer, Jin-Ha saw it was Grant Hartwig. He must have forgotten something.

To Jin-Ha's surprise, he came over to where she was standing. Jin-Ha found she couldn't move.

He looked at her.

"You have ice on your face," he said. His voice was the voice of the rough boy, the one who'd called her a math geek—and worse.

"What's it to you?" Jin-Ha said. She tried to make her voice sound mean, but it only dribbled out pathetic and sad.

"You been crying?"

To Jin-Ha's horror, she felt like she was going to start crying all over again. Her eyes and nose got hot, but she held her breath and squeezed her chest, and thankfully, the tears went back in.

"It's not good to cry in this weather," Grant said, as if he were lecturing her. "Your eyes might freeze shut, and you'd have to stay that way until spring."

Jin-Ha knew that wasn't true. It was almost funny, but she didn't feel like laughing.

"Hey," he said, "I wanted to say I'm sorry." It was suddenly the voice of the boy who picked up her books for her. Jin-Ha looked up in surprise.

"I'm sorry I said . . . that," he said. "I shouldn't have called you a math geek, and you know, the other thing. I'm not a racist, you know."

Jin-Ha wanted to tell him that he *was* a racist, but all she could do was hiccup.

"Well, I just wanted to say sorry," Grant said, knocking some snow off one boot with the other. "I told my friends they'd better not say that kind of stuff to you any more, either. We act pretty stupid when we're together."

"You're not stupid in math," Jin-Ha wanted to say, and to her surprise—she did.

"Thanks," he said, and smiled. "Well, gotta go. See you around in math class, huh?"

He didn't wait for her to say anything, but walked away, his blue jacket receding into the black night.

Jin-Ha turned to go back inside. She wiped hard at her face with her scratchy mittens. Too many strange things had happened tonight, and it was all because of Grant Hartwig. Wasn't there a book she had read—*Dr. Jekyll and Mr. Hyde?*—about a man who takes some kind of formula so he's one way part of the time, and the opposite the other half of the time? Grant was like that, and it was confusing her.

* * *

"Jin-Ha," Deanna said proudly, when she walked back to their table, "Maggie finished her report! And she showed it to me; it's pretty good, too."

"Good for you!" Jin-Ha said, smiling. The last of the ice was melting on her cheeks. It felt good to smile, she realized.

14

When Jin-Ha came home the next evening, there was a familiar, but somehow forgotten, smell in the house—like seeing a friend whose face you know well but whose name you've forgotten because it's been so long. It took her a second.

Beef, sesame oil, soy sauce, green onions.

"Bulgogi!" Jin-Ha said excitedly. *"You made bulgogi!"* She ran into the kitchen to give her mother a hug.

"It's not real bulgogi," her mother said. *"The sesame oil here doesn't taste the same as changirum."* She showed Jin-Ha the oil bottle. Indeed, the color of the oil was golden, not the rich brown color of *changirum*, Korean sesame oil.

"It smells great to me," Jin-Ha declared. She washed her hands and started setting the table.

When her father came home a few minutes later,

they all settled down to a meal of rice, *kimchi*, lettuce, and grilled meat. *Bulgogi* needed to be sliced very thin to cook properly, so you had to buy expensive meat that was tender but lean. Jin-Ha couldn't remember the last time they had a meal this fancy.

"What's the occasion?" she said, as she began wrapping a piece of meat in a lettuce leaf.

Her parents exchanged happy looks. Jin-Ha wondered if her father had gotten a raise. Or maybe he had been promoted to mechanic!

"The occasion is you, of course," her mother said, smiling at her. *"We're so proud of you for doing well in school. We knew it would be hard for you, starting in a new country and a new language, but you've done so well, even in the hardest classes!"*

Jin-Ha gulped, a lump of rice stuck in her throat. She coughed.

"Are you all right?" her father asked, patting her between the shoulderblades. Jin-Ha sputtered a few times.

"I'm fine," she said. *"It just went down the wrong pipe."*

Ooooh, she was thinking. Her parents spent carefully-saved money to make *bulgogi* to celebrate her F? How could that be?

"You are our fabuloso daughter," Jin-Ha's mother said, and her father looked on approvingly, as if he were impressed by Jin-Ha's mother's knowledge of idiomatic English.

Jin-Ha knew she needed to say something. Otherwise, it was just going to get worse and worse. A lie was like mold: it kept growing and growing no matter how much you tried to keep it down. Soon, it would be in places you couldn't reach, hiding where you couldn't see it.

But how should she tell her parents that their daughter was a *liar* as well as a stone-head? Jin-Ha felt her food grow cold in her stomach. If only she had studied harder, this wouldn't have happened. Or, if only she'd refused to take that stupid honors class—she'd probably be doing fine right now. Why should she always do whatever someone else told her to? Wasn't she the best judge of herself?

"This is delicious," her father said, looking at her mother.

"Thank you," she said.

"Your English is getting as good as your cooking. Soon you'll sound like a real American, like our bright daughter here."

Jin-Ha's mother blushed and smiled. She seemed like her old self again, like Shim Cheong, the one who tackled anything with a calm ferocity, not the lady who was afraid to speak English in front of strangers.

Jin-Ha kept shoveling food in her mouth, even though she couldn't taste it anymore. Her mother had probably spent all afternoon shopping for, slicing, and marinating the *bulgogi*. Her father had worked for hours under some dirty, drippy car to earn the money. And right now they looked so happy. She should let them stay happy, shouldn't she? What could she do?

The only solution she could think of was to study, study, study. From now on, she was going to study full speed, one hundred ten percent, no, two hundred percent—harder than she ever had before. She would stay up all night if necessary and get her grade back. That way her parents could go right on being happy, and no one would ever have to know anything had gone wrong.

"Have more," her mother said, dishing the last succulent piece of meat onto her rice.

"Oh no, *Appa* should have it," she said.

"No, you take it," her father said, waving her off. "You're the scholar of the family. You know, at first I was very disappointed not to be able to teach college—no one at Jack & Don's has a master's degree, you know—but I see you're going to do all right. So being here *is* a good thing because you can take advantage of America's wonderful educational system much earlier than I did.

"Are you glad we moved here, yobo?" he said to Jin-Ha's mother. He only called her *yobo*, honey, on special occasions. Usually it made her mother blush, but now she glanced at Jin-Ha and nodded happily.

Jin-Ha felt like shrinking as she forced the last piece down. She didn't look at her parents, but she knew they were both smiling at her.

15

The next day in math class, Jin-Ha handed in her homework. She had copied most of the answers out of the back—that was the best she could do. She had also rehearsed something many times this morning and was ready to say it.

"Uh, Mr. Arneson?" she said. He stopped collecting the papers and looked at her. "I had some trouble with this chapter. Is it possible that you could review it a little before we go on?"

Mr. Arneson peered at her.

"You're having trouble with *polynomials?*" he said unbelievingly.

Jin-Ha felt like hiding. She nodded.

"It's all quite basic," he said with a huff, as he went to the blackboard with the half-collected homeworks still in his hand. He made a quick scrawl of two polynomials on the board joined by a multiplication sign.

"See it's just first, inside, outside, last," he said, tapping the chalk loudly on the blackboard. "How much easier can it get? I could explain it until I'm blue in the face, la-dee-da."

Jin-Ha scrawled the example in her notes. First, inside, outside, last, she chanted to herself. When she got home and reviewed the homework, would it work? she wondered.

"Okayyyyyyyy?" Mr. Arneson said, in a tone of voice that meant "It better be okay."

"Okay," Jin-Ha said, in her timid voice. Shim Cheong was nowhere to be found.

Jin-Ha sat miserably through class. When the bell finally rang, she got up promptly.

"Having a little trouble with polynomials, huh?" Grant Hartwig was behind her, making his way to the door as well.

It was the nice-Grant voice.

"I'm having trouble with everything related to math," Jin-Ha found herself saying, as they joined the stream of kids changing classes.

"It's not that bad, polynomials, really," he said. "It isn't that much different than working with single numbers, when you get down to it."

"Really?" Jin-Ha said. "Then why can't I get it?"

"Maybe you just need to look at it differently," Grant said. His eyes suddenly started scanning the hall, and he began to move away from Jin-Ha.

"Come to the library tonight," he said, not looking at her. "If you want some help."

"Hey!" A crowd of hockey players suddenly descended on him. "It's Grant Fartwig! The big fart-man pee-yoo!"

"Shut up, Pizza-zit-face," he said in a rough voice that Jin-Ha knew very well. He was lost in a flurry of backslaps and guffaws. Jin-Ha made sure to go the other way.

"So, do you want to go to the library tonight?" Maggie asked Jin-Ha on the phone. "My mom says she can take us."

Jin-Ha wondered which Grant would be there: the nice or the evil Grant? After what had happened the last time she was at the library, she almost didn't want to go. But what if he was there, and helped her with math? She needed to be like Shim Cheong, facing unknown dangers.

"I'd love to go," she told Maggie.

"I'll be out late—don't bother waiting up," Jin-Ha's father said to her mother. He was going to walk Jin-Ha and her friends to the library and then go to his class.

"Okay," her mother said, but to Jin-Ha, her voice seemed to be teetering on the edge of a sigh. At first Jin-Ha thought her mother would be glad he was gone so much since it gave her a lot of time to work on the sweater. But maybe the house would seem empty and cold if you were alone and couldn't even watch TV since it was all in too-fast *jeet-jeet* English. And it was true that he'd gone out almost every night this week—wasn't that a little strange? Jin-Ha decided she'd try to come home early and keep her mother company.

"Study hard," her mother called to Jin-Ha as they walked out the door.

*   *   *

As soon as they arrived, Jin-Ha found herself scanning the room to see if Grant would really be there.

"Jin-Ha, over here." Grant was sitting at a table by himself. Maggie's eyes opened wide when she saw him. Deanna's did, too.

"Well, I, uh, Grant said he'd help me with my math."

"Him?" said Deanna unbelievingly.

"Him?" said Maggie, a bit dreamily. "Well, we'll wait for you over here at our usual table." Maggie and Deanna made a big show of moving to the other side of the library.

Jin-Ha went to the table where Grant was sitting and put down her books. So he really was here. But might it be a trick? Some kind of mean prank? Were the other hockey players hiding someplace, laughing? Would they all come out and yell "chink!" at the same time?

Grant opened his book.

"Okay," he said. "Do you want to start with polynomials, or something farther back? I, um, noticed you didn't get the best grades on some of the tests."

Jin-Ha blushed furiously. She had hidden the tests back in her desk drawer: she didn't want anyone—least of all Grant—to think she was dumb.

"Well, I am having some problems. I mean, that's why I need to study," she said, swallowing her pride. "I think once I study everything will be fine."

"Okay, then let's start." He pulled out his test paper. He'd only gotten one wrong!

"I think part of your problem might be the way Arneson teaches," he went on. "He's a lousy teacher. He just talks at us and never shows us why the concepts work the way they do."

Jin-Ha was shocked. Even though she agreed with Grant's every word, she would never say so out loud. In Korea you would never criticize an adult, much less a *teacher*.

"So let's look at this story problem with the coins. It's pretty straightforward if you know how to set up the variables."

He pulled out a piece of paper and started to outline the problem.

"See, you just have to remember that the number of coins is a function of the total sum, right?" Grant dug out some coins and put them on the table. "So the number of the coins times their values equals the sum, right?"

"I see," said Jin-Ha. "I think."

"Here," Grant said. "This problem in the book is a lot like the coin problem. Why don't you try it on your own?"

"Okay," Jin-Ha said. It was funny how when she wasn't so nervous, the problem didn't seem quite so imposing.

"Hey," Grant said a few minutes later. "I think you've got it."

"It's pretty easy once you explained it," Jin-Ha admitted. "You're really good at math."

He blew his bangs out of his eyes with a puff of air. Grant was one of the few boys in the school who had brown, not blond, hair. "When I was a little kid, I used to keep stats for the hockey team. Partly I liked it because I got to spend time with my dad. And partly I liked making all the numbers come out right—you know, one plus one equals two and nothing else. The funny thing was, my dad had me do it to learn hockey, not math. I started getting really into math after that, and I think he was a little bummed by it."

Jin-Ha realized that she'd never really *looked* at Grant before. In her mind he was just a big boy with a blue jacket, big hands, a mean face, and a loud voice. He still had big hands and a blue jacket, but his face wasn't mean. It was actually rather pleasing: he had nice skin, the color of the inside of a seashell, with a dusting of about three freckles on each side. He looked the way she thought the young groom who saved Black Beauty might look.

Grant leaned back in his chair, stretched, took a deep breath, and sighed.

"For once I can study math out in the open and not up in the stacks," he said. "What a relief."

"I don't understand," Jin-Ha said.

"Well, like I said, my dad's not crazy about my interest in math. When I study at home, after like five minutes he'll say I'm studying too much and I'll weaken my eyes and I'll have to wear glasses like supernerd, which will ruin my hockey, and blah-bitty blah. But if I go to the library and study, my friends say I'm a fem if they see me studying at all. That's why I usually go up to the stacks. But tonight my friends aren't here."

"What's a fem?" Jin-Ha asked. Another idiomatic expression?

Grant looked at her in surprise. "You really don't know? Well, it's not a good word," he said. "Mostly, it means that you act like a girl."

"What could be bad about acting like a girl?" Jin-Ha asked. "Girls *and* boys should study. You need to study hard to get into college, and you need to go to college if you want a good job. In Korea, kids start studying when they're little—I had homework when I was five."

"There's plenty of stuff you can do without going to college," Grant said. "But yeah, I'll admit I *like* math. It's like a hobby. But my dad wants me to just play hockey. Actually, everyone's at practice right now."

"So why aren't you there?"

He shrugged. "I'm a little burned out on hockey this year," he said. "And besides, I thought I'd give you some help to make up for all the times I was mean to you."

"So you quit?" Jin-Ha asked.

"No. Once I got to practice I told my dad I was feeling sick and instead of going home I came here. He's the high school coach, but he helps out the junior high coach on Wednesday nights."

"You lied to him?"

"It's not exactly a *lie*. I just don't want to tell him I'm tired of hockey. I think he'd be really disappointed in me."

"But next time, are you going to make another excuse, too?" Jin-Ha asked.

"There's not gonna be a next time," Grant said roughly. He pulled out his test paper again. "Okay, let's look at the binomial theorem. Now, don't let the fact that there's an X *and* a Y scare you . . ."

It wasn't quite mean Grant on the loose again, but it wasn't exactly nice Grant, either, Jin-Ha thought.

But Grant was a good teacher, Jin-Ha had to admit. He knew how to break things down and explain them. And when he drew pictures, he did it slowly, so you could see what he was doing. He even rearranged Mr.

Arneson's "first, inside, outside, last" binomial theorem formula to "first, outside, inside, last"—which spelled F-O-I-L.

"Wow, it's so much easier to remember this way," Jin-Ha marveled.

"And the outcome is exactly the same," Grant added. "I don't know why Mr. Arneson makes things so hard. Or why he doesn't explain better."

"Whew, I think I'm actually getting this," Jin-Ha said. "Now I can go home and study on my own. Before, I couldn't even study because I had no idea what was going on."

"Did you know that our book has the answers to the homework in the back?" Grant asked.

"Oh, yeah," Jin-Ha said, a little guiltily.

"Well, you can use it to your advantage."

"Oh, yeah?" Jin-Ha couldn't believe Grant would need to copy the answers to the homework, too.

"Sometimes if I'm a little lost, I look at the answer *first*."

"You do?"

"Yeah, because sometimes if I can't work out a problem going forward, I can figure it out going backward. Kind of like in *Jeopardy!* where they give you the answer and you have to come up with the question."

"Oh, I love *Jeopardy!*," Jin-Ha said. What Grant said made sense to her.

"And also," Grant went on, "you can practice on the problems Arneson doesn't assign. Every once in a while, he puts problems from the book on the tests because he's so lazy."

"How do you know?" Jin-Ha said.

"I do extra problems if I'm bored," Grant said, but

then he turned away a little, as if he thought that Jin-Ha, too, might think he was weird or a "fem" for liking math so much.

"That's great," Jin-Ha said, and meant it. "I feel exactly the same way about my science class. I do extra reports all the time—if I had my way, I'd just take science classes."

They were quiet for a few seconds. Jin-Ha knew there was something she had to ask him. She needed to be like Shim Cheong and not be afraid to take a jump into the icy sea.

"Grant, can I ask you something?"

"Sure," he said. "But do I have to answer?"

Jin-Ha forged on. "Remember when I first came to school, and you called me a 'chink'?"

Grant winced.

"And then after that you stole my egg from my lunch and played baseball with it in front of the whole lunchroom?"

"Yes," he said, reluctantly.

"I didn't even know what a 'chink' was," Jin-Ha went on. "We don't have a word for that in Korean. But anyways, after I found out it was a bad word, I felt really awful. Now I want to know, why would someone who's as smart as you do something like that?"

Grant squirmed. "Well, first, I'm not smart," he said. "In fact, I'm dumb. My grades except for math aren't all that great, and I do dumb things, and I don't know why. Well, actually, I do know why."

"Why?" Jin-Ha said.

"Because I'm a guy and that's what guys do," he said, sounding a little annoyed. "You do something dumb, and someone else does something dumber, and you do

94

something even dumber. You know how girls talk about other girls for fun? Well, guys do dumb things for fun."

"But why do you do *mean* things?" Jin-Ha asked. "Like picking on people, stuff like that?"

"Jeez," Grant said. "We do mean things to *each other* all the time, no big deal. That's how guys are. You have to prove that you can dish it out and take it, too. That's what being cool is all about. You have to be tough. It's like hockey; you might get smashed into the boards, but my dad says you can't complain, you just have to go and check the other guy even harder."

Jin-Ha sighed. "If that's true, then I'd rather not be cool."

Grant shrugged.

"You said yourself you're not a bad person," Jin-Ha said. "So why don't you just act more like your real self? Maybe the other guys will, too, and they'll stop doing stuff like calling you Grant Fartwig."

Grant blinked. Then he closed his book. "Well, I think we're pretty set now. Any questions?"

Jin-Ha had many more questions for Grant: Why there was a Jekyll Grant and a Hyde Grant, a mean boy and someone who'd spend a whole hour helping her with math? Did he mind it when the boys called him names? If so, why did he turn around so easily and call other people names? Was the solution to getting hit always to hit back harder? Of course, those questions weren't the kind of questions he was referring to.

"I guess I'm okay," was what she finally said. "I understand it a hundred times better."

"That's good. I gotta go," he said hoisting his duffel bag, which was blue and also said NORBUHL BLUEJACKETS HOCKEY on it. "See ya."

95

Jin-Ha suddenly wished he would stay, talk more. But she didn't know how to ask him to stay. She raised her hand and said, "Thanks for the help, Grant." It came out in her timid voice, and she wasn't sure if he heard.

"OhmyGod," Maggie said, when Jin-Ha came back to their table. "What was that all about? You didn't tell us you had a study *date* with Grant Hartwig."

"It wasn't a date," Jin-Ha said. She could feel herself blushing. "He felt bad about the book mixup and stuff, so he offered to help me with math just this once."

"*He* helped *you?*" Deanna said. "That's like Einstein getting homework help from Hulk Hogan. Like Marie Curie getting help from Barney the prehistoric purple eggplant."

"He's actually pretty smart in math," Jin-Ha said. "You know that test I flunked? He only got one wrong."

"Is he still here?" Maggie, looking around hopefully. "Are his friends going to meet him here?"

"The rest of them are at hockey practice," Jin-Ha said.

Maggie's face fell. "Why can't I get a hockey player to help me with *my* homework?" she lamented.

"So why wasn't he at practice?" Deanna asked. "Especially since he's Mr. Big-Shot-I-Am-God-No-I-Am-Better-Than-God Joe Hartwig's brother."

"I'm not sure," Jin-Ha said.

"Well, maybe there's hope for everyone," Deanna said. "He spent a whole evening studying instead of bashing people over the head with a stick. Maybe next he'll discover the virtues of PBS—you never know."

"Hockey's a very difficult sport," Maggie said with a little sniff. "It requires a lot of skill and precision."

Deanna smiled at her. "Yes, I suppose you have to *aim* your stick at the other guy's head."

"Deanna! I'll have you know that bashing people over the head is *not allowed*. It's called 'high sticking.' "

"I'm just kidding, Maggs," Deanna said. "Don't forget that my brother Jamie played bantam-A, too. I just think it's funny that you stick up for hockey more than those guys probably do."

"Someone's got to do it," Maggie said. "I was actually thinking of trying out to be the team's statistician when I get to high school."

"You'd probably be great at it," said Jin-Ha.

"But Jin-Ha, you're so lu-cky!" Maggie exclaimed, looking at Jin-Ha's pile of notes. "Grant even wrote stuff down for you."

Jin-Ha looked down at the pieces of paper Grant had left her with. She liked Grant's squared-off handwriting. It looked so confident. F-O-I-L. One plus one equals two, and not three, or anything else . . .

"Bet you're going to keep those papers under your pillow," said Maggie.

"Guess so," Jin-Ha said. She would do anything to conquer the math monster and regain the trust of her parents.

16

Jin-Ha set her alarm clock for six the next morning. Its weird quacking noise startled her out of her dream earlier than she thought possible. It was so dark she couldn't see her hand in front of her face—it had to be a mistake. She looked at the glowing numbers of her clock. 6:01, it read.

Jin-Ha hopped over to her desk and wrapped herself in a quilt, trying her best to draw her feet up into its pod of warmth. She opened her math book and pulled Grant's papers from under her pillow. "The binomial theorem," the top one read. She looked it over again, and then began studying.

She almost fell asleep again at 6:45, but by then she had done half her homework problems and hadn't looked at the answers in the back *once*.

*   *   *

"Jin-Ha-yah! Time for breakfast. Don't be late for school!" Jin-Ha's mother's voice roused her. She lifted her head off the book. It was almost 7:45. Oh no! No time for a shower this morning. She ran to the bathroom.

Jin-Ha was very tired that day, but in math class, she confidently took notes. She actually understood what was going on! Of course, this was thanks to Grant, not Mr. Arneson, but who cared how you learned as long as you learned, right?

After class, she looked over at Grant to see if he'd say hi, talk to her. But he just pushed right past her and, once he was in the hall, disappeared.

"Ooog, I'm so tired," Jin-Ha complained at lunch.

"Why?" Maggie asked.

"Because I got up early this morning to study for math. It really helped, though. I got all my homework done, and I wasn't as lost in class as I usually am."

"Why not sleep in and just let Grant help you more?"

"I don't think so," Jin-Ha said. "I think that was just a one-time thing. Anyway, I need to learn how to do it on my own."

"Wow," Maggie sighed. "I can't believe you were sitting with Grant Hartwig last night. Did you sit on the same side of the table or opposite sides?"

"Maggie!" Deanna said. "Stop pestering Jin-Ha for all these irrelevant details."

"What's 'irrelevant'?" Maggie asked.

"It means it doesn't have anything to do with anything," Deanna replied.

"Irrevelant," Jin-Ha said. She liked that word. "Maggie, I can't even remember who sat where, so I guess that does make it irrelevant."

"It's relevant to me," Maggie said, getting up and throwing her brown bag in the trash. Jin-Ha and Deanna followed her. "How else can we find out if he likes you or not?"

"Oh, please." Deanna laughed. Jin-Ha did, too.

"Deanna."

The three girls turned. Charlie Muller, an eighth grader, was behind them, following them out of the lunchroom. His face was red, and he looked like he was sweating. Jin-Ha wondered if maybe he was sick.

"Hey, Charlie."

"Hi, Charles," said Maggie, batting her eyes.

"Uh, Deanna, I gotta ask you something."

"Shoot."

"Not here."

"Why not?" Deanna said, annoyed. "We need to go to the girls' room before class, so we haven't got all day."

"I'll ask you by the drinking fountain."

"Oh, hmph," said Deanna. "All right, but this better not take long. Wait for me, will you?" she said to Maggie and Jin-Ha.

Deanna and Charlie went over to the drinking fountain. Maggie and Jin-Ha didn't know what else to do, so they watched. Charlie coughed a few times, Deanna got a drink. Then she came back, smiling a big smile.

"What was that all about?" demanded Maggie. "Charles Muller is an *eighth grader*."

"I've known him since like kindergarten; it's no big deal," said Deanna, and then she smiled even more broadly. "So he asked me to the Christmas dance."

"Really?" said Jin-Ha, in awe. She had no idea Deanna would be the first one to go on a date with a boy.

"So what did you say?" asked Maggie.

"Well, I thought about it for like two seconds, and then I said, 'Why not?' I like to dance."

"Oooh, you're so lucky," Maggie said. "Here you don't even like any guys and you get a date for the dance, and Jin-Ha gets Grant Hartwig to help her with her math!"

"That's the secret," Deanna said, and she was grinning. "Don't like the guy you want to like. To me, Charlie has always been the dorky red-headed neighbor boy who looks like Howdy Doody—although I admit he's gotten a little better with age—and Jin-Ha certainly didn't have any crushes on Grant Hartwig."

"That's for sure," said Jin-Ha, although listening to Deanna's story made her wonder if there was a possibility that Grant, too, might get better with age.

"So what should I do?" Maggie sighed. "I like everyone. I guess I'll have to wait for the results of my test."

"What test?" asked Jin-Ha and Deanna at the same time.

"You'll see," Maggie said mysteriously.

*

"Oh no," Maggie said. "I screwed up."

They were sitting at Maggie's house, and Maggie was nervously deconstructing a pile of Oreos but not eating any of them. She stacked the disks up in front of her as if they were black poker chips.

"What do you mean?" Jin-Ha asked. She kept her watch on the table so she would know to leave in plenty of time to go home and study.

"This." Maggie shoved a test at her and Deanna. There was a D-minus at the top.

"Oh no!" Jin-Ha said. This was just like what had happened to her! "Was the test really hard?"

"No, actually, it was too easy," Maggie said. "I just filled in a few answers, but they were all correct, so Mr. Janovich gave me a D-minus—can you believe it?"

"But you're good in math," Jin-Ha said.

"Wait a minute," Deanna said, reaching out to look at the test more closely. "You mean you were *trying* to get a bad grade?"

"Just this once," Maggie said. "Joel Carlson is in my class, and I thought maybe he'd want to help me with my math." She looked meaningfully over at Jin-Ha.

Deanna groaned. "Magdalena Racquelle Josephs, don't tell me you did what I think you did."

"Do what?" Maggie said.

"Deliberately bomb the test."

"I'm not great at math," Maggie protested. "See, I didn't get picked for honors math, either."

"You should have been—and that's not the point. Up until now you were getting an A in there."

"One bad grade won't mess me up, then."

"But why deliberately do that? To impress boys? I can't think of anything more *stupid*!"

There was a small silence.

Maggie looked down. She played with her fingers a little before she spoke. And when she did, her voice came out quiet, much quieter than usual.

"But you got asked to the dance. And Grant will ask Jin-Ha, I bet. Then I won't have anyone. I know it's stupid, but I'll feel awful if you guys all go to the dance and I stay home."

"Oh, Maggie," Jin-Ha said. She was afraid that Deanna might have hurt her feelings, even though she didn't mean to. When Deanna got excited, she often said things you could take in a bad way if you didn't think about why she was saying what she was saying.

"Deanna didn't mean *you're* stupid," Jin-Ha said. "She was just pointing out how grades are important. My parents are always telling me that I might not think grades are important, but they are, and I probably won't realize it until it's too late—like when I can't get into college or something. We both know you're very smart, right, Deanna?"

Deanna nodded, looking a little sheepish.

"Yeah, I didn't mean it like that, Maggs," she said. "I just mean you have to be true to yourself. Lots of people would kill to be as smart as you."

"Hm, I guess," Maggie said slowly. "Jeri got good grades *and* she had boyfriends."

Jeri was Maggie's older sister, Jerilyn.

"See?" Deanna said. "Jeri had lots of boyfriends, and I'll bet she has tons in college, now, too. And she didn't even have to go around calling herself Jerilyn all the time."

"But we can call you Magdalena if you want," Jin-Ha added. "I just keep forgetting because we've called you Maggie for so long."

"Nah," Maggie said. "Keep calling me Maggie. Your father and my mother are about the only people who call me Magdalena, and then I'm like, 'Huh? Who're they talking to?' "

The girls laughed and put their hands out for a group squeeze.

17

"And you see that by moving the X over to this side you now have a straightforward set of variables. You could also achieve the same effect by inverting the X the other way, but then you have to remember that in that situation there's a possibility that X could be a negative number, which means this number would turn into a minus, but the other number is also minus, so it would be minus a minus, which turns into a plus. Plus a minus, of course, would still be a minus, as you see here. But then, if it's a positive number, it's just business as usual, plus and minus."

Jin-Ha tried to concentrate extra hard on what Mr. Arneson was saying, but it made her head ache. She had reviewed today's lesson last night to make absolutely sure she'd be ready, but it didn't seem to make much difference. Mr. Arneson's monotone swept over her like an ocean wave.

She was losing it, losing it, lost again.

She felt like raising her hand and asking a question, but she didn't know what to ask. And if she asked him to slow down, he would probably get upset again. She looked desperately over at Grant. He looked scowly, as if he disapproved of every word Mr. Arneson was saying. He didn't look back at her.

Mr. Arneson zoomed on, declaring, like a magician announcing his next trick, that he was now going to prove the problem by drawing a diagram. His chalk went all over the board, drawing arrows and A's and B's, fluttering, the way her father's pen did when he drew intricate calligraphy characters.

"There and there," he said, pointing to the lines on the board with his chalk—tok!-tok!-tok!—leaving white dots all over the place. "You see?"

Jin-Ha didn't see. She just wanted to go home.

Jin-Ha noticed Karen Norgaard scratching her head as she sat at her desk, even though the bell had rung.

"Do you think this class is hard?" Jin-Ha asked her, as she passed her desk.

Karen continued scratching her head.

"It's getting harder," she said. "But I think I'm still hanging in there."

"Um, maybe you would like to study together some time or something? You can come over to my house if you like."

Karen got up, unfolding her long limbs like a stork. She was tall, but had terrible posture, Jin-Ha noticed.

"I don't really make it my business to study with other people," she said, her voice just this side of snippy. She strode into the hall, and Jin-Ha followed her.

"Besides, my brother was in this class two years ago and still has all his notes."

"Oh," said Jin-Ha, disappointed. "So you use your brother's notes?"

"Of course. I have to—do you think anyone catches all of what Mr. Arneson says in class? He's such a rambly-mouth dork who drinks too much coffee—peeyoo, have you ever smelled his breath?

Jin-Ha cringed. She wasn't used to all this teacher-criticizing. But even if it was Mr. Arneson, not math, that was her problem, it didn't help the situation at hand. She would do anything to be able to study with Karen, look over her brother's notes. But that didn't seem very likely, did it?

"Your father had to go out," Jin-Ha's mother told her when she got home. *"But we need some groceries, so let's go to the super."*

"Okay," Jin-Ha said.

At the WinkyDinky, Jin-Ha grabbed a handbasket instead of a cart because they didn't want to buy more than they could easily carry home. As they turned up the cereal aisle, Jin-Ha noticed a man standing in the middle of the aisle, comparing two boxes of cereal. As they neared, Jin-Ha saw he had Lucky Charms in one hand and Trix in the other. Jin-Ha thought the Lucky Charms would be a better choice for the man because "Trix are for kids."

When the man turned his head a little, Jin-Ha saw that it was Mr. Arneson.

Jin-Ha held in her gasp. Mr. Arneson was completely absorbed in comparing the two boxes, one showing a rabbit, the other, a leprechaun. To Jin-Ha's relief, he kept staring at the boxes, and she and her mother walked undetected, right behind his back and down the aisle.

"Gina!"

She almost groaned out loud. She thought about pretending not to hear, but then she decided that probably wouldn't work. She stopped and turned around.

Mr. Arneson must have put the Lucky Charms back on the shelf because only the Trix was in his cart. The rest of the stuff was all prepared foods: cans of Spaghetti-Os, TV dinners, potato chips with the dip flavor already built in, microwave popcorn.

"Hello!" he said, as if they were long-lost friends. "Is this your mother?"

"Uh, yes," she said. Her heart was pounding so that she could barely think: what if he said something about her F's? She turned to her mother and said reluctantly. *"Mom, this is Mr. Arneson, my math teacher."*

"Hello," Jin-Ha's mother said, bowing slightly. "It is nice to meet you."

"Ditto," said Mr. Arneson.

Jin-Ha's mother looked at her, waiting for the translation. *"He said 'it is nice to meet you, too,'"* Jin-Ha said.

Jin-Ha's mother didn't seem convinced that "ditto" could equal "It-is-nice-to-meet-you-too," but Jin-Ha didn't know how else to translate such an idiomatic expression. At the same time, Mr. Arneson was eyeing them as if they were talking about him in some top-secret code. Why couldn't he have kept staring at the cereal for two seconds longer? Jin-Ha lamented.

"Well, no need to be talking about school outside of

school," Mr. Arneson said. "But Gina, I hope you'll be working hard the next few weeks to improve your grade. This is junior high honors math, you know; it's not elementary school any more."

"*What did he say?*" her mother said immediately.

"*He said . . .*" Jin-Ha shifted the handbasket from one hand to the other. "*He said we have some big tests coming up and I need to study hard.*"

"*Of course,*" her mother said.

Mr. Arneson grasped the handle of his cart. "And like I said before, you have a natural advantage. You Japanese are going to beat our butts—oops, excuse the language— if we're not careful."

"*So now what did he say?*" Jin-Ha's mother asked. "*I thought I heard him say something about the Japanese.*"

Jin-Ha shrugged. How to translate that? How could Mr. Arneson think they were Japanese, with a name like "Kim"? Koreans always have short names like "Lee" or "Park," while the Japanese usually have long names like "Miyamoto" or "Fukiyama." For a teacher, he sure wasn't very smart. "*He just talked about math, and how the Japanese school system is supposed to be so good at teaching math.*"

"*Your teacher is absolutely right,*" her mother said. "*The Japanese do have a good school system. What a smart man.*"

Jin-Ha wondered what her mother would say if she told her what Mr. Arneson *really* said.

"Well, it's time to finish my shopping," Mr. Arneson said, starting to wheel his cart away. "See you in class, Gina. Nice meeting you, Mrs. Kim."

"Nice meeting you, too," Jin-Ha's mother said.

*   *   *

Jin-Ha, Deanna, and Maggie settled themselves at their usual table.

"Darn," said Maggie, looking around. "The hockey players aren't here."

"Like Jin-Ha said, they're at practice," said Deanna. "We can start doing our homework at the rink, if you'd like."

"Ha-ha, very funny," said Maggie. "I just like having a little scenery when I do my homework."

Jin-Ha pulled out her report on bees and decided to start with that. She hoped doing something she liked would put her in a better frame of mind for untangling her math notes.

But unfortunately, when she finally started working on her math, it was as confusing as ever. How could she be so lost again already? She tried doing the problems backward, starting from the answer in the back the way Grant had shown her, but she was beginning to suspect that might be hopeless, too.

Out of the corner of her eye, Jin-Ha thought she saw a blue shape move past them.

"Look," Maggie hissed. "Grant Hartwig is here!"

Sure enough, Grant was at the other end of the room. He propped his hockey duffel on the other seat as if it were a person and opened a book with an orange cover— their math book, most likely. Again, he was alone.

Jin-Ha wondered if he'd help her one more time. As much as she hated to ask him, she really needed his help. Mr. Arneson had said they were going to have three or four more tests this marking period, but there was only

18

"Yobo," Jin-Ha's mother said to her father at dinner, "today I met Jin-Ha's math teacher."

Jin-Ha tried not to groan out loud.

"And what kind of fellow is he?" her father asked.

"He seemed very nice. And he said lots of nice things about our daughter."

"Of course, that's only fitting." Jin-Ha's father beamed at her.

"Mr. Arneson isn't that great," Jin-Ha said to her father. "He's not that smart when it comes to things outside of math. For instance, he thinks we're Japanese."

"Well, that's natural," he answered. "People around here don't have too much experience with Asian people. When I was at the University of Minnesota in Duluth, people were always asking me if I was Chinese or Japanese—Korean wasn't even one of the choices!" He ex-

plained this quickly in Korean to Jin-Ha's mother, and they both laughed, but Jin-Ha didn't.

"Mr. Arneson is also not a very good teacher," Jin-Ha went on. "No one in class understands the lessons."

"Jin-Ha," he went on, "never criticize your teacher. A teacher knows more than you do, you know."

"But you told me you always called your elementary school teacher 'Mr. Tiger' because he was so mean," Jin-Ha protested.

"That's right," her father said. "And in fact once my friends and I were giggling about it in the bathroom—and who was hiding in there, but Mr. Tiger himself! We got roundly whipped for that, I recall, and we had to clean the toilets for a month. What a stench!"

The phone rang. Jin-Ha's father picked it up.

"Hello?" he said, and then frowned, which made Jin-Ha wonder if it was someone selling something again.

Or, Jin-Ha thought in a sudden panic, what if it was Mr. Arneson calling about her grade?

"Hi, Magdalena, I think the battery is low on your phone," he said. "Jin-Ha is right here, but we're eating, so please make it quick." He handed the phone to Jin-Ha.

"Jin," said Maggie, in between some static, "want to go to the library tonight? Mom's bridge game is at Mrs. Lindstrom's house, so she can pick us up and drop us off, no sweat." Maggie spoke so fast, she panted at the end of the last sentence.

"Okay," Jin-Ha said. She was realizing that according to their schedule, they would be having a math test very soon, so she might as well study at the library. "And Deanna?"

"I'm calling her next. See you at seven—bye!"

a little more than two weeks left before Christmas—so that meant they would be having a lot of tests very soon.

Jin-Ha screwed up her courage and decided to ask for help.

"Hi, Grant," she said, as she walked to his table.

"Hi, Jin-Ha," he said, and waited for her to continue.

"Um," she said, "are you doing your math right now?"

Grant looked up at her. "What does it look like I'm doing?" He sounded slightly annoyed, and Jin-Ha tried not to melt. Think Shim Cheong, think math grade! she told herself.

"I'm lost again," she said. "And we're going to have a test really soon because Mr. Arneson said we're going to have at least three tests before the end of the marking period and if I don't do well my parents will be really disappointed!"

Jin-Ha hadn't meant to say all that, but it had somehow all tumbled out of her mouth.

"So you're asking me to help you?" Grant stared at her.

"Well, yes," Jin-Ha said.

To her surprise, he smiled.

"You can ask me any time." He pulled out the chair next to him. "Have a seat."

Jin-Ha gingerly sat down. She was so close to him, she could smell the fresh laundry detergent smell from his clothes. A relevant detail? she was wondering.

"I just started the homework," Grant said. "So why don't we begin there? Okay, we have the X here, so if we multiply it here—"

"But in the problem he did today, he divided it," Jin-Ha cut in.

"No, he makes you *think* you should divide to keep X on this side. But it's easier just to invert and *multiply* X, right? If you want to divide one-half by one-half, it's just easier to invert and multiply one-half by two, don't you think? You get absolutely the same thing—try it."

"Um," Jin-Ha said. "Right, I guess." Grant's way of looking at a problem was so opposite to Mr. Arneson's method. Mr. Arneson just said something was the way it was and to memorize it. But Grant actually gave her the tools to solve the problem, and she could use what she learned on other problems.

"You should be a math teacher," Jin-Ha said.

Grant grinned. "Think so?"

"Definitely."

"I like making math easier for other people," he admitted. "Haha, although some teachers we know seem to like to make math harder for people. We won't name names."

"Did you have hockey practice again tonight?" Jin-Ha asked.

"Yeah," he said.

"I thought you said there wasn't going to be a next time," Jin-Ha said, before she thought of how bold it might sound.

Grant shrugged. "At the time I said it I thought that. I forgot about the math tests coming up—I need time to study, too, you know. I just wanted some time alone, maybe."

"But what did you tell your dad this time?"

"Same thing, stomach hurts."

"Maybe you should start telling him the truth," Jin-Ha suggested.

"That is the truth." His voice was the mean-Grant's

voice now, but somehow, Jin-Ha wasn't scared of it any-more. "My stomach *does* hurt."

"But if you hate hockey, just quit. If you like math, and want more time to study math, do that. Join the math club."

Grant pounded his fist on the table. "No way I'd be a math-club geek," he said. "What a bunch of fems!"

Jin-Ha winced. "You said yourself 'fem' was a bad word, like 'chink.' "

Grant stopped, but his mouth was still moving, as if he were swallowing words, silently gargling them.

"Sorry about the word," he said finally. "But I don't think you understand. Math club is for geeks and I wouldn't join it if you put a gun to my head. And hockey. I'm *good* at hockey. People say I'm even better than my brother when he was my age—and my brother was awesome."

"But if you don't like it—" Jin-Ha said.

"I do like it—most of the time. I guess it's just differ-ent than when I was really little. Then, I just batted the puck on the ice. Now, my dad is already bugging me about getting a college scholarship just like he did. And he thinks I'm gonna turn pro. I'm in seventh grade! Maybe my brother doesn't mind being a hockey robot, but I kind of do."

"Where is your brother now?" Jin-Ha asked.

"Playing hockey in college, on a scholarship."

"Oh, wow," Jin-Ha said, impressed. Grant's brother must be very smart as well.

"Well, he's not really playing right now," Grant said. "He got injured at the last game."

"What happened?"

"Some guy on the other team checked him really hard and the guy's skate sliced into his leg."

"Oh, my," said Jin-Ha.

"Yeah, it was bad," Grant said. "The guy hit him so hard the doctor was taking pieces of *sock* out of his leg. When you play, you wear these thick socks, you know."

"So is your brother in the hospital?"

"He's at home right now. He's dying to hit the ice again."

"But will he be able to play again?"

Grant shrugged. "He says so. I'm sure he will. I mean, hockey is his whole life. He doesn't have a lot of hobbies, he's not that smart. He'd better be able to play."

"But you said he got a scholarship," Jin-Ha said. "He must be smart."

"He got a scholarship to play *hockey*. That just means you get all A's in shooting goals. In school, to Joe, a D is a good grade. I think most of his professors must be hockey fans because he hasn't failed anything yet."

"Oh, my," Jin-Ha said again.

"Oh, my is right," said Grant. "So do you get the stuff, now?"

"I think so." Jin-Ha sighed. Grant had cleared things up for her, but, she wondered, for how long? Would it last long enough for her to do well on all three tests?

"Well, hope you do okay on the test," he said. "You catch on pretty fast."

"Thanks," Jin-Ha said, getting up. The Jekyll and Hyde Grant seemed to be merging into one person.

"So did he ask you to the dance?" Maggie asked, when Jin-Ha came back.

"What?" said Jin-Ha. "Why would he want to do that?"

"Like—duh—because he likes you?"

"I don't think so, Maggie," Jin-Ha said. "I asked him to help me with my math."

"But why does he hang out here, when he knows we come to the library almost every night? When he has practice? And with his math book?" Maggie said. "Jeez! He probably thinks you're not interested. That book says you have to let boys *know* you like them."

"Maggs," said Deanna, "I think Jin-Ha is more interested in her grade in math than in Grant Hartwig."

"Huh—who says you can't be both?" said Maggie. "And *you* have a date for the dance."

"So why don't *you* ask someone?" Deanna inquired.

"No way!" Maggie almost exploded. "That violates rule number one—you wait for the guy to ask, *then* you show interest. That's why Jin-Ha needs to pick up the ball when Grant is sending such clear signals. Now, I made the mistake of bombing my math test, and then I found out that practically all the guys in the class did worse than me including Joel Carlson, who flunked his—how could that be? The test was so *easy.*"

"Maggie, don't sacrifice grades for boys," Jin-Ha cautioned. "Joel Carlson might look cute now, but it's not worth it."

"Yeah," Deanna added. "With a brain like that, he'll probably end up working at McDonald's or be an auto repair jockey or something—oops!" Deanna looked at Jin-Ha, and then clapped her hand over her mouth.

"Oh my God, Jin-Ha," she said, from behind her hand. "I didn't mean it like that. I mean, your dad has an education and all."

"You and your big mouth," said Maggie. "Deanna, you might want to try thinking *before* you speak, for a change."

Jin-Ha let everything settle around her for a second. Her father did work at a car repair place; that was nothing to be ashamed of. But she didn't think Deanna meant it that way, either.

"That's okay," Jin-Ha told her. "That's true. Even though my dad likes working at Jack & Don's well enough, my parents want me to go to college so I *won't* have to do stuff like that. In Korea, my dad would be a respected teacher. But because he wants to be here, he sort of has to start all over. Even just to teach community college or high school here he has to go to school some more."

"I'm very sorry, though," Deanna said. "I didn't mean to be mean. I didn't mean it like that."

"I know you didn't," Jin-Ha said, patting her friend's arm. Then she grinned at her. "You're just lucky I know what you mean when you say something like that."

"Yeah, I am lucky," Deanna said. Jin-Ha noticed that she was looking enviously at her math notes, the page filled with X's and Y's.

19

Mr. Arneson gave them a test, unannounced, on Friday.

"I did say we were going to have at least three tests, maybe four, before the end of the marking period, didn't I?" He tsked-tsked as he licked his fingers to pass out the test. Karen Norgaard glowered at him and chewed on her pencil.

Jin-Ha didn't have any energy to waste on getting mad at Mr. Arneson. As soon as she got her test, she bent her head down and attacked it.

Everything went well until the end. There was a story problem about two trains meeting each other at some point X (wouldn't they crash?). She drew a picture. She put the X on the other side, as Grant had shown her, but that didn't work, either. Finally, she assembled the problem as best she could and made a guess.

*   *   *

"What did you think of the test?" Grant asked, as they walked out of class.

"I don't know," Jin-Ha said. "I hope I did well enough to pull up my grade."

"Well, no one can say you didn't study."

"But that problem about the trains gave me some trouble," she said.

"Oh yeah," Grant recalled, glancing down the hall. "Mr. Arneson didn't really explain that concept in class."

Joel Carlson and some of the hockey players were walking their way. Jin-Ha wondered what Grant would do.

"Well, study hard for the next one," he said, walking away from her.

"It's the big blue whale!" she heard him yell as he joined his friends.

"You look hungry," her mother said, when Jin-Ha came home. *"Would you like some kimchi and rice? A sandwich?"*

"No thanks," Jin-Ha said. *"Mom, I have something to tell you."*

Her mother looked at her quizzically.

"M-my grades. They're not very good. The one in math, that is."

"What are you trying to say?" Jin-Ha's mother said.

"My-my grade. The fabuloso *one? It's—it's—"*

Her mother smiled tenderly at her. *"I think you must have studied too hard in school today,"* she said. *"Why don't you take a rest? Go play outside."*

"But math—math—" Jin-Ha sputtered. *"The fab-fabuloso . . . it's not, it's not. . . ."*

"Yes, I already heard your teacher say you're doing well

120

in his class, so don't worry. Ah yes, I need to buy some buttons for your father's sweater—why don't we take a walk together?"

Jin-Ha didn't know what else to do, so she accompanied her mother to That Yarn Cat. The lady with the silvery bun was behind the counter.

"How's the sweater going?" she asked.

"Pretty well," Jin-Ha said. "Now we need some buttons."

"Okey-doke. Let me show you what we have. I think for that sweater, some wooden buttons might be nice."

Jin-Ha's mother barely said anything the whole time they were at the yarn store, even though the lady asked her questions in a very clear voice: Did she like this button, or that one? Bigger? Smaller? How many? Mostly, her mother just shook her head, nodded, or held up a number of fingers.

When they left, the yarn lady gave them a hearty "Good-bye!"

"Good-bye," Jin-Ha's mother replied, in a soft voice, to Jin-Ha's surprise. Maybe she was starting to trust the yarn lady, Jin-Ha thought, cautiously happy for her.

Maybe if her mother was in an environment with all nice people, she would relax enough to start speaking English again, Jin-Ha thought with sudden inspiration. What if she took a class, like Jin-Ha's father was doing? The community college was always advertising "enrichment" classes like dancing, computers, or literature that you could take for fun. Jin-Ha knew that her mother liked to learn, and if she had some American friends to see in a class, she'd be less lonely and could practice her English at the same time. Jin-Ha decided she would bring up the community college idea at the next opportunity.

"Oh, *look*," said her mother, pointing in the window of Verna's Bakery. Right now, in the cold air, a warm smell of fresh bread and cookies delighted their noses.

"*What are you pointing at?*" said Jin-Ha.

"*Those.*" Jin-Ha looked. Her mother was pointing at some pastries baked in the shape of a triangle.

"*They're like the ones at Nari Bakery,*" Jin-Ha said. The bakery by their house in Korea was called Nari Bakery because the woman who owned it was named Nari. Jin-Ha's mother's favorite pastries were triangles filled either with sweet bean paste or melted brown cinnamon sugar.

"*I don't think these are filled with sweet bean paste, though,*" Jin-Ha said. "*Americans don't eat beans for dessert like we do.*"

"*But they do look just like them—isn't that something?*" said her mother. Jin-Ha thought she looked "wistful"; she had just learned that word in English class. The teacher explained it as "longing for a person, a place, or a time that was far away." Jin-Ha's mother was longing for these baked pillows, which were breadlike on the outside and sweet on the inside and oh, so far away.

20

The next day, they got their tests back.

Jin-Ha carefully turned hers over.

Eighty-eight and one-half, a B-plus. She had gotten every answer right except the story problem; Mr. Arneson had given her half a point for setting it up. Eighty-eight wasn't an awful grade, but she needed to do better.

"Merry Christmas, students," said Mr. Arneson. "Ho ho ho."

Pinned to Mr. Arneson's tie was a plastic Santa head. To Jin-Ha, its pink plastic cheeks and red-lipped smile looked gruesome.

"Okay, class, you're getting a present: I'm going to treat you like adults."

"Yay," said some of the kids, clapping, but they didn't know what they were clapping about. Jin-Ha just sat there. It sounded to her like Mr. Arneson was just being tricky again.

"Instead of the two or three more tests you're supposed to have, you'll only have *one* more. Of course, this next test will be worth a lot more, since we're only having one. So you'll have to study hard. The big enchilada test equals three of our normal little taco tests."

Jin-Ha groaned.

"The test will be next Thursday," Mr. Arneson said. He pulled on the string hanging from the Santa pin, where Santa's neck would have been. The red nose blinked on and off nervously.

"But that's the day after the Christmas dance," someone protested.

"So?" Mr. Arneson was ready for that. "Do you expect the world to work itself around your personal schedule?"

Mr. Arneson twirled his mustache and smiled. Jin-Ha could see more and more why he would buy Trix. Did he decide to combine the tests because he was so lazy? she wondered. He would have fewer tests to type up and a lot fewer to grade.

But what did it mean for her? Maybe it would be better—she could get the whole thing over with at once. But somehow, the prospect of scaling one huge mountain seemed much more formidable than two or three smaller ones.

*

That night after dinner, Jin-Ha's father went out again. This week, again, he'd been out more nights than he'd been in. Jin-Ha noticed her mother had that anxious look again.

124

"Are you worried about something?" Jin-Ha asked her, after he'd gone out.

"Well." Her mother made her knitting hands work fast, until they became a blur of fingers, yarn, and needles. The ball of yarn jerked spasmodically as it grew smaller and smaller. *"I hope your father's not working too hard. He spends so little time at home these days."*

"Dad is strong," Jin-Ha said, but she wondered if maybe it would be better not to talk more about it. Jin-Ha did think it was a little strange that a class would have her father going out almost every night of the week, but how could she inquire about it without sounding suspicious of him?

"Mom, did you ever think about taking a class yourself, maybe at the community college?" Jin-Ha asked.

"Why would I want to do that?" her mother said.

"I'm talking about a fun class, like learning how to dance or something. You could meet people that way. And you could improve your English. Maybe you could take an English class."

Her mother put down her knitting and looked at her.

"Are you ashamed of me not speaking English?" she asked.

"Oh, no, that's not it at all," Jin-Ha said. She could never be ashamed of her mother. *"I just thought that might make you happier."*

"What makes you think I'm not happy?"

Jin-Ha was worried that her mother was upset with her, but she saw a bit of a smile playing at the corner of her mouth.

"I didn't say you're unhappy," Jin-Ha said, trying to choose her words carefully. *"I just thought it must be boring sitting here all day when Dad and I are gone."*

Her mother picked up her knitting again.

"Well, it is a little hard," she admitted. *"We don't really have anyone here."*

"I know," Jin-Ha said. *"Wouldn't it be nice if Imo and Halmoni could live near us?"*

Jin-Ha's mother nodded, and she looked sad. Jin-Ha was suddenly realizing that she couldn't remember the last time they'd talked to *Imo* or *Halmoni*. Calling Korea was frightfully expensive and the time zones were so different—when it was one o'clock in the afternoon in Minnesota on a Tuesday, it was four in the morning on *Wednesday* in Korea.

"Is it hard to make friends here?" Jin-Ha asked.

"Everything is rolled together," her mother said. *"When you're young, like you, you are like fresh new elastic—you can learn and do new things and spring back good as new. When you get older, like your mother, you're more brittle—and you have to be afraid of going too far and breaking. Things come slower, like language. And if I can't speak English, it's hard for me to make friends and do other things."*

"I see," Jin-Ha said thoughtfully. *"Is there anything I can do to help you?"*

Her mother smiled, then looked down at her knitting, counting the rows.

"Just study hard. Here, I'll get you some fruit." Jin-Ha's mother got up to go to the kitchen. Jin-Ha realized she still hadn't answered her question about the community college, but she decided she'd better start studying.

When Jin-Ha's father came home, Jin-Ha noticed that a sharp smell of smoke came in with him.

"What's this smell of smoke?" Jin-Ha's mother asked him, as she took his coat. Jin-Ha's father didn't smoke.

Jin-Ha's father paused.

"There were a lot of people smoking in class," he explained. *"Sorry it went on for so long."*

Jin-Ha's mother took a deep breath, as if she was going to sigh, but she held it in. Jin-Ha's father hung up his coat. Jin-Ha went back to her studies, feeling a little strange and praying that nothing was wrong. What kind of school was it where students smoked in class? Jin-Ha wondered.

21

Burt Humphrey, the goalie of the hockey team, asked Maggie to the dance. He had marched right up to her at lunch and asked, just like that.

"Aren't you excited?" Deanna asked. "All your studying—of that dating book, that is—paid off. A-plus."

"I don't know," Maggie said. "I wasn't interested in him—he just sort of came out of the blue."

"Excuse me," said Deanna, cupping her hand to her ear. "Who was it I heard lamenting she didn't have a date for the dance?"

"But what's the use of getting guys you're not interested in?" Maggie sighed. "Besides, you know what the other guys call him?"

"What?"

Maggie sighed again. "The Blue Whale."

Jin-Ha and Deanna laughed. They couldn't help it.

Burt was big, in a kind of round-shouldered, round-stomached way, and, like all those boys did, he wore his big blue NORBUHL BLUEJACKETS HOCKEY jacket twenty-four hours a day. It clung to him like plastic wrap on a melon; so, yeah, he did look like a big blue whale.

"They probably aren't saying that to be mean," Deanna said. "It's probably because they like him. Everyone knows that boys don't mature as fast as girls, so instead of just saying, 'Hey, you're cool,' guys come up with things like 'You're a big poopy pants jerkface' to say they like you."

"And you want to go to the dance, don't you?" Jin-Ha added.

"I guess," Maggie said. "Jin-Ha, why don't you ask Grant and we can all go?"

"Grant?" Jin-Ha said. "Why would I want to go to a dance with *him*? Besides, I have to study for that math test—*and* I don't think my parents would let me date yet."

"This really isn't a date kind of thing," Deanna said. "The whole school will be there, and they'll have teacher chaperons."

"Well, they're against boy-girl stuff in general."

"You've got to be kidding," Maggie said. "We're in seventh grade!"

"It's different in Korea. After you're seven years old, you're supposed to ignore boys. You don't date until you're in college, and even then your parents check everyone out. In fact, there's this thing called a *son poda* where they just go ahead and pick the person for you. My parents met that way, through my mother's aunt. They met at a coffee shop with my mom's mom and the aunt right there. They saw each other like two more

times to meet all the relatives, and then they got mar-
ried—poof! Just like that."

"No way!" Maggie exploded. "They never got to go
on dates? I'd die."

"But that's not necessarily a bad idea—parents already know what their kids are like," Deanna commented. "And look at Jin-Ha's parents. They have a
really happy marriage."

Jin-Ha thought of her father going out so much lately,
and of her mother's sad, anxious face. Before this, she
would have totally agreed with Deanna. Now she wasn't
so sure.

*

The next week was an awful one for Jin-Ha. She had
a test in English and she had to memorize the 206 bones
in the human body for science. And of course the big
math test was staring over her shoulder, wherever she
went.

"How's your studying going?" Grant asked her, when
they met in math class.

"Okay," Jin-Ha said.

"That's good." Jin-Ha couldn't believe that the same
boy who was so mean to her in the library now seemed
almost concerned about what kind of grade she was going
to get.

"Are you going to the dance?" Grant said suddenly.

"No," Jin-Ha said back. "Why?"

Grant twiddled his thumbs and watched them, as if
they were the most fascinating things in the world.

"Just curious," he said.

Jin-Ha wondered for a second if Grant was meaning
to ask her to the dance. She felt strangely happy just to
be asked, to be picked by someone, even though there

was no earthly way she could say yes, between her math test and her parents. But if he was, why didn't he just come out and ask? Maggie and Deanna's dates didn't seem to have any problem.

Karen Norgaard came into the classroom, walked between them, and plunked her books down on her desk.

"How's the hockey season going?" she said to Grant, almost flirtatiously. He mumbled something.

Jin-Ha went to her seat and sat down. In any case, math was the important thing, and she had to keep remembering that.

*

That night, Jin-Ha's father wasn't home by six, as he usually was. Jin-Ha noticed that her mother paced around anxiously, looking toward the front door every few minutes.

The doorbell rang.

"I hope it's your father," Jin-Ha's mother said. *"The food's going to get cold."*

Jin-Ha ran to open the door. When she did, she gasped. There was her father, along with a green friend who was taller than he was: a big bushy pine tree.

"Merry Christmas," said her father.

"You got a tree," Jin-Ha exclaimed, jumping up and down. "A Christmas tree!"

Her father carried it inside. "It was so big that Jack had to tie it to the top of his tow truck to get it here."

Jin-Ha's mother came to see the tree. The worry had melted from her face, and she was smiling.

"Aigu," she said. *"It's so beautiful!"*

"Our Christmas tree," said Jin-Ha's father. *"In English, this kind of tree is called a* pine tree."

"Pine-oo tree," Jin-Ha's mother repeated.

"Jin-Ha, run to the Hokanssons' and see if they have an extra tree stand," her father instructed.

Jin-Ha came back with a metal stand. Jin-Ha's father set the tree in it and poured some water in the basin. He showed Jin-Ha how to refill it and told her to never let it go dry because the tree was thirsty and needed a lot of water. If they gave it enough water, he said, the tree would stay beautiful for weeks. Jin-Ha gazed up at it. A few soft branches touched the ceiling, and a beautiful smell of pine pervaded the room.

"This is our Christmas present from Boss Jack," said Jin-Ha's father.

"The pine smell is nice," Jin-Ha's mother said.

"How should we decorate it?" Jin-Ha wondered. *"We don't have any ornaments."* Then she felt bad for saying it. She knew what her parents would say: she should be grateful for a tree, and here she was worrying about decorations.

But her parents just smiled. *"We'll think of something fabuloso,"* her mother said. *"We're a creative family."*

132

22

Jin-Ha tried to study the way Grant had suggested: doing the problems Mr. Arneson hadn't assigned and then checking the answers in the back. She got up early in the morning and did problems, and she did them late at night, too.

"Ah, my little mathematician," her mother said proudly, noting the open math book, as she brought Jin-Ha some fruit. If she only knew, Jin-Ha thought.

*

"I'm bummed you can't come to the dance," Maggie said when she met Jin-Ha and Deanna the next morning. "My mom's taking Deanna and me to the mall after school to get some fun earrings to wear tonight. Want to come?"

"No thanks," Jin-Ha said. "I have that big math test tomorrow."

"Well, I'm sorry you're missing the dance, Jin. Stuff like the Christmas dance only comes once a year—we'll miss you!"

"Don't worry," Jin-Ha said. "We'll have plenty of fun together once I get this grade straightened out." And, she promised herself, she was *never* going to let things get this bad again.

*

"Class," said Mr. Arneson, just as the bell was going to ring. "I know that tomorrow is the day of your test, but we do have a little rearranging of the schedule to do."

Jin-Ha's heart leapt. Maybe they would have a few more days to study!

"I was looking at the schedule and realized there's no possible way to cover chapter thirteen by tomorrow."

"Yay!"

"Uh-uh-uh." Mr. Arneson wagged his finger at the students who'd cheered. "I would appreciate it if you would let me finish. What I'm saying is that you're just going to have to learn chapter thirteen on your own."

BBBBBBRing!

People slammed their books on their desks and mumbled angry things. Jin-Ha was numb. What was she going to *do*?

After school, she worked straight through on her math. Chapter 13, to her horror, was almost all story problems! It was about the probability of a certain number coming up, for instance, if you rolled some dice. You had to figure out a formula to predict it, but she had no idea how to get that formula, and the book's explanation was so confusing. She panicked, thinking how, on the last test, missing that one story problem was enough to send her grade plummeting from an A-plus to a B-plus. What could she do?

There was only one thing she could do, she decided. She dug out the phonebook and looked under "Hartwig." Grant could teach himself the material and then teach it to her. There was a Grant K. Hartwig on Highland Street listed. Grant must be named after his father, Jin-Ha thought.

She waited until her mother went to the bathroom. Then, strangely fearless like Shim Cheong, she dialed.

"Hello," she said to the lady who answered. "May I please speak with Grant?"

"Big or little Grant?"

"Little." She wanted to giggle, despite herself—it was hard to think of Grant as "little."

"Hello?"

"Hi, Grant, it's Jin-Ha from school."

"Oh, hey," he said. His voice was casual, as if they talked on the phone all the time. "What's up?"

"I have a big, big favor to ask you," she said. "I have to talk fast. I'm having a lot of trouble with chapter thirteen. Can we meet for a few minutes at the library tonight?"

"No problemo," he said. "I was thinking of swinging by there anyways."

"Oh, thank you!" she said. She was so relieved.

"Dad, are you going out tonight? I need to go to the library," Jin-Ha asked her father at dinner.

"Yes, I do have an extra study class tonight," he said.

"I'm sorry, you'll have to get a ride with one of your friends."

"Okay, I'll ask Maggie or Deanna," Jin-Ha said. She would call them after dinner. She made a mental note to herself.

Wait! The dance was tonight!

"Um, excuse me for a second," she said, getting up.

"Jin-Ha, aren't you feeling well?" her mother said, concerned.

"I feel fine," Jin-Ha said. *"I just need to call someone."*

"Jin-Ha, we're eating," her father said. "Call after dinner."

"But it's important," Jin-Ha said, trying not to let her panic show.

"Unless someone's house is on fire, or if they're otherwise in danger, it can wait," her father said. "So, is this person's house on fire?"

"No." Jin-Ha miserably sat back down. What could she do? The mound of food on her plate now seemed impossibly huge. What if she couldn't meet Grant?

How she wished they had a car! Everyone else's family had a car, *two* cars, actually. In fact, Deanna's family had three—her older brother Jamie had his own souped-up Mustang. And why was her father going out so much? Didn't he like spending time with her and her mother? He didn't even seem guilty or sad, he just trooped out the door and didn't come back until her bedtime. He would never do that in Korea—over there, once he was home, he was home. Was America changing him?

Eat, she told herself. *So you can call.*

Her stomach hurt from eating too fast, but Jin-Ha finally finished, excused herself, and dragged the phone into a closet.

"Deanna," she said, when her friend got on the phone.

"Jin-Ha?" said Deanna. "What's up? Your voice sounds all weird, like you're calling from Timbuktu."

"I'm in the closet. Deanna, I need to go to the library tonight because Grant is going to help me with math and I really need his help. But my dad's going out. What should I do?"

"Uh-oh, we have the dance tonight," Deanna said. "We'll be leaving pretty soon."

"I *know*," Jin-Ha said. "Help me figure something out—please!"

"Okay, okay, I'll think of something," Deanna said. "Hm—let me call Maggie and see if she has any ideas—hold on."

"Okay," Jin-Ha said. "Hurry!"

In only about three minutes, the phone rang.

"Deanna?" Jin-Ha said.

"Jin-Ha?" It was a boy's voice, not a girl's. "It's Grant."

"Oh, Grant," she said. "I was just thinking about you."

"You were?" Jin-Ha was surprised at how pleased he sounded. "I was thinking about you, too."

"What about?" Jin-Ha asked.

"Maybe we should go to the dance."

"What?" said Jin-Ha. "We have to study."

"Oh, to *study*, of course," Grant said. "But tonight's practice has been canceled so the hockey players can go to the dance, and my dad'll think I'm lame if I go to the library instead."

"But how can we study at the dance?" said Jin-Ha. "Won't it be noisy and dark and full of kids?"

"It's going to be at the Elks Club because the gym has water damage. There'll be lots of quiet places to study," Grant said. "My dad is a member—I've been there before."

Hm, Jin-Ha thought. This situation was a little strange: go to the dance to study? But then again, maybe she could get a ride with Maggie and Deanna . . .

"I'm waiting for a call from Deanna," Jin-Ha said. "Let me talk to her first and I'll call you back."

As soon as she hung up the phone, it rang again. It was Deanna.

"Jin-Ha? What's up? Your line's been busy."

"I know," Jin-Ha said. "Have you guys thought of anything?"

"Yes, we have an idea—actually, it's Maggie's idea. Have Grant meet you at the dance and talk there—I'm sure you can find a sorta quiet place," Deanna said. "It's not a hundred-percent perfect solution, but this way you'll have a ride there and back."

"Grant had that same idea," Jin-Ha said.

"He did? Okay, then, that'll probably work. We'll be by at seven."

Jin-Ha realized she had one more problem: what to tell her parents. What would they think about a school dance with *boys* there? Of course, there would be teachers there, but what if they still said no? She'd just have to risk it and go without telling them where she was going. Anyway, she'd be back home on time, just as if she'd gone to the library.

Jin-Ha put her books in her bookbag and went into the living room. Her mother was at the kitchen table. She was wearing her winter coat, which wasn't so strange because it was very chilly in the apartment, but Jin-Ha thought she saw her tuck something into her right sleeve.

"What's that?" Jin-Ha said.

"What is what?" said her mother. She pointed at her book bag. *"Aren't you staying home tonight?"*

"I need to go to the library. Is it okay if I go? There are some books I desperately need. Maggie's mother said she'd pick me up and Deanna's mother will bring me back."

"Okay," her mother said, looking small in the light of the kitchen. *"If you have to study you have to study."*

"After all these tests, it'll be Christmas break and we'll have lots of time to do fun things together," Jin-Ha promised her mother as she pulled on her shoes. *"And we'll have the best Christmas!"*

"Yes," her mother agreed.

When Jin-Ha spied the headlights of Maggie's mother's car pulling into the parking lot of their building, she breathed a big sigh of relief. This was going to work after all. She was going to study so hard that she would never, ever have to lie to her parents again.

23

The Elks Club had the head of a big dead elk—horns and all—hanging over the entrance.

"Oh, ugh, would you look at that?" said Maggie. Even as they walked inside, the dead elk seemed to keep its glassy stare on them.

THIS WAY TO THE NORBUHL JUNIOR HIGH DANCE read a sign with a hand pointing down the hall. WEDNESDAY NITE BINGO said another sign next to a room where people were setting up rows of chairs and tables. On the other side of the hall was a dark room lit only by a dim hanging lamp that said GRAIN BELT BEER, and Jin-Ha could just make out shapes of men and women drinking together.

The room the dance was in was even darker. The girls could make out streamers at the front entrance, but that was about it.

"Ooog," said Deanna, as they walked inside. "Scary. I feel like I'm walking into a cave or something. Hellooooooo. Where are the bats?"

"Hmf," said Maggie. "Joel Carlson is here with Lori Langstrom—can you believe it?"

Jin-Ha squinted. "I can't see a thing."

Somewhere in the dark, a round figure was moving toward them, like a whale gliding among a bunch of shrimps.

"Hi," Burt said to Maggie. "When'd you get here?" There was a thin sheen of perspiration on his face. He was in his good clothes: polo shirt, corduroys that had a neat crease down the center.

"Just got here," Maggie said, looking around.

"Well, let's cut a rug," he said, extending his elbow.

Cut a rug? Jin-Ha was thinking. That was certainly an idiomatic expression she'd never learned before.

"Cut a rug?" Deanna broke in. "What the heck is *that?*"

Burt chuckled. "That's how my grandfather asks my grandmother to dance. Sometimes when Lawrence Welk is on, he puts his elbow out to my Gramma"—he stuck his elbow out again—"and goes, 'Hey Mom, let's cut a rug.' "

"Your grandfather calls your grandmother 'Mom'?" Jin-Ha asked.

"Ya, it's his pet name for her. She calls him 'dad.' "

"And they dance in the living room?" Maggie asked with horror, as if Burt were explaining some weird Transylvanian custom involving blood and raw meat.

"Ya," he said. "And hey, we don't even have a rug in the living room—it's wall-to-wall carpeting."

"Oh, whatever," Maggie said. "I'm thirsty. Where's

the punch?" Maggie disappeared into the dark with Burt following her.

A few minutes later, Charlie Muller came for Deanna. She tried to act casual, but Jin-Ha could see—or maybe feel—her blushing, even in this dim light.

"You go on ahead," Jin-Ha said. "I'll wait for Grant."

"Are you sure?" Deanna said. "I don't mind waiting."

"Go ahead," Jin-Ha said, hoisting her book bag on her shoulder. "A good song's on."

"This is a good song," Charlie agreed. So Deanna went off, and Jin-Ha was alone. She didn't mind. It was fascinating to watch. In Korea, they could never have dances like this in middle school. First, the Plum Flower school was all girls. And Jin-Ha couldn't believe that couples actually touched while they danced—with her English teacher and her homeroom teacher standing right there!

Then Jin-Ha saw something that shocked her even more. Some kids were running around with magic wands that had glow-in-the-dark stars on top. When they tapped couples on their heads, they were supposed to kiss—and most of the time they did.

Now that her eyes had adjusted to the dark, Jin-Ha realized she'd never seen a kiss so close up before, except maybe on TV or in the movies. She had never seen her parents kiss, not even a peck on the cheek the way Maggie's mom and dad did when they said hello or goodbye.

And these were *real* kisses. The boys' and girls' mouths were clamped together like fish mouths, moving, opening and closing, gulping and swallowing. Jin-Ha was fascinated and grossed out at the same time.

"Hey, Jin-Ha."

Jin-Ha turned around. Grant was standing a little

ways away, as if he wasn't sure he wanted people to know he was talking to her. He had a shopping bag from Blue Ribbon Sports looped over his wrist and a plastic cup of punch in each hand.

"I found a good place to study," he said, pointing a cup of punch toward the exit door. "Follow me. I already told Deanna where it is."

Jin-Ha followed him out of the dark and the music to a lounge that had a TV with some comfy chairs surrounding it, as well as a table with folding chairs. Grant put the cups down on the table.

There were a few older men watching TV—a Western complete with cowboys and Indians—and they just smiled at Grant and Jin-Ha.

Jin-Ha and Grant smiled back. Even with the TV on, this room was ten times quieter—and brighter—than the dance hall.

Grant opened the Blue Ribbon Sports bag and took out his math book. "Chapter thirteen?"

"I tried studying it on my own, but I just couldn't get it," she said.

"Okay," Grant said. "Let's take a look."

Four cups of punch later, they had done all of the problems in the chapter. At least chapter 13 was short.

"Okay, here's a test—try multiplying this polynomial," Grant said, writing something down. Jin-Ha stared at the problem. It was longer than any one she'd ever seen, but she thought F-O-I-L, and solved it.

"Wow, you've done a lot of studying," Grant said.

"I need to get an A," Jin-Ha said, explaining the "F is for fabuloso" problem and all the trouble it had caused.

"I guess the lesson is, you shouldn't have lied in the

first place," Grant said. Then he added, "Although I'm not a great role model for that."

"Well, if I get an A on this test, they'll never have to know," Jin-Ha said.

"What do you want to be when you grow up?" Grant suddenly asked her.

"Oh, I don't know." Jin-Ha took a sip of her punch. "A zillion things: marine biologist, doctor, astronaut, maybe a teacher. My parents both say I would be a good doctor, since I'm good at science, but I think you have to be good in math, too. How about you?"

Grant twiddled his thumbs. "I don't know," he said. "Like I said, my dad wants me to be a professional hockey player. Either my brother Joe or I have to be one, he says."

"But you said your brother already wants to be one, didn't you?" Jin-Ha said.

"Yeah, but he's got his injury. That's why all of a sudden the pressure's on me."

"But you said it'll get better," Jin-Ha replied.

"No, everyone *hopes* it'll get better."

"Do you even *like* hockey?" Jin-Ha asked. "Sometimes it seems like you don't."

"Me? Who knows?" Grant said. "My dad started me on skates before I could walk. Now it's practically more natural for me to have skates on than shoes. I *think* I like hockey a lot, I do. It's just that it's changed so much since I was a little kid playing on the rink by my house. Now it's all about competition, who does the most scoring, what position you play. Even if we play a good game, my dad gets all upset if we lose. That's not fun for anyone."

"Wow," Jin-Ha said. "Your father is as passionate about hockey as my parents are about grades."

"I sure wouldn't mind it if my parents cared about my grades—or anything that didn't have to do with hockey, for a change. Joe, he's so dumb I used to have to help *him* with his math. You'd think my parents would be worried about that, but they weren't."

"What about Joe? Didn't that bug him?"

"Nah," Grant said. "He's like my dad, says once he's a big hockey star he'll just buy a bunch of calculators. But then if he doesn't make it to the pros, what's he going to do?"

"I don't know," Jin-Ha said. She was beginning to see why getting good grades was important. It seemed longer-lasting than the ability to be good on skates.

"Hey, guys." Deanna came in. Her cheeks were rosy, and the little curls in her bangs were pasted flat onto her forehead with sweat. "I just wanted to remind Jin-Ha that my mom'll be here at nine forty-five."

"Okay, thanks," Jin-Ha said. She moved to start cleaning up. Tomorrow was make-or-break day. She hoped she had studied enough.

Grant made sure to hide his book carefully in the shopping bag before they went back to the dance floor. Jin-Ha recognized the song that was playing—she had listened to it in Maggie's room: "Your eyes make me sad thinking of the times we never had . . ."

It was a lonely song. She liked it because it reminded her of a sad Korean folk song.

"How about a dance?" said Grant.

"Huh?" said Jin-Ha in disbelief. "A dance? With you?"

"It won't be *that* awful, will it?" said Grant.

"Oh, I didn't mean it that way," said Jin-Ha. But she had never thought of Grant as a boy. Well, not that much, at least.

"So let's dance. We can't come to the school dance and not dance one dance, you know."

"Hm," Jin-Ha said. She did like the song. And it wasn't as if dancing were wrong: Look, there were tons of teachers here. But what would her parents say? Would they be against dancing? They would certainly say she should be polite—and wouldn't it be polite to dance with someone who had asked her?

"Oh, okay," Jin-Ha said, putting down her book bag.

Of course, Jin-Ha had no idea how to dance. Her friends in Korea, Kyung-Hee and Ji-Sun, said they knew all the dances from watching music videos on TV, but Jin-Ha had no clue. All the other couples were swaying together like seaweed in a gentle ocean current. Jin-Ha tried to follow Grant's movement, but she seemed to be constantly a beat behind.

"Here," said Grant, putting her hand on his shoulder. "Just follow my feet."

Jin-Ha had never been so close to a boy before, and it made her nervous. She almost breathed a loud sigh of relief when the song changed to a faster one. She gratefully stepped away from him and danced alone.

"Jin-Ha, you're dancing!"

It was Maggie and Deanna with their dates. They came over and they all began dancing in a big group. Maggie and Deanna danced exactly the way the three of them danced when they were in Maggie's bedroom. Jin-Ha could do that.

"Hey," Maggie yelled, over the music. "I'll show you

how to do the Loose Caboose." She started shuffling her feet and sliding her hips. Jin-Ha copied her and so did Deanna. Soon, the three of them were doing a synchronized dance together.

The lights came on right after the last song was done. After blinking for a few seconds, Jin-Ha saw that the floor was littered with fallen streamers, snowflake cutouts, an abandoned wand. The teachers looked tired.

"Looks like it was a successful dance," Grant commented. Jin-Ha realized they were visible to everyone, including the other hockey players, who were making their usual noise. But Grant waved offhandedly to a few of his friends and continued to walk with her.

"Aren't you going with your friends?" she asked.

"I will," Grant said. "After I make sure you find your ride."

Deanna and Maggie had gone to the coat check, so Jin-Ha and Grant walked to the front by themselves. On their way out, they passed the bingo room. People were sitting in the chairs, intently hunched over their bingo cards.

Her father.

All of a sudden, Jin-Ha thought she saw him. She thought he came out of the dark room—the bar—passed her, and walked down the hall into the men's room.

And it seemed like he saw her, too. His eyebrows flew up like birds, even as he ducked into the men's room. The whole incident took maybe three seconds.

Jin-Ha began to wonder if she had just hallucinated: What were the chances her father would be in the Elks Club when he was in a class across town at the community college?

"Are you okay?" said Grant. From another room, Jin-Ha could hear a booming voice say, "And the next round will begin in five minutes. Pick up your new cards at the front table."

"I don't know," Jin-Ha said.

"You look sick," he said. "Do you need to sit down?"

"No," Jin-Ha said. She didn't know what to think, what to do. How could that have possibly been her father? But how many other Korean men were there in Norbuhl? And of course she knew her own father's face! So was that him? What was he doing in the bar? Was he doing something bad, like seeing another lady, drinking, or gambling?

She stared at the men's room door, hoping the person she thought was her father would come out and explain, but he didn't. Then she wondered how she would explain to her father why she was in the Elks Club after she had told her parents she was going to the *library?* She gulped.

"We'd better go," she said to Grant. "Deanna's mom's probably waiting."

Jin-Ha and Grant found Deanna and Maggie out front.

"Well, good luck on the test tomorrow," he said. "I think you'll do fine."

"Thanks for your help," Jin-Ha said.

"Any time," Grant said. "I mean that. Well, see you. Bye, Maggie, Deanna." He walked back into the club, the elk's head over the door wordlessly watching him go.

"OhmyGod," said Maggie. "He is, like, so fabuloso-ly polite."

Deanna didn't disagree, and neither did Jin-Ha. Despite all the weird things that had happened tonight, she realized she had liked dancing with him.

Deanna's mom showed up a few minutes later. When Maggie crawled into the tiny car, Jin-Ha noted that she was wearing Burt's big hockey jacket under her coat. It was so big it hung way below the hem of the coat. As they rode home, Maggie told them about how she and Burt had been slow dancing when the people with the glow-in-the-dark wands showed up. Jin-Ha looked over at Deanna, who was sitting quietly. She was all smiles, as well.

"Hi, Mom," Jin-Ha said, when she arrived home.

Her mother looked up from her knitting. "See, it's almost done," she said. Indeed, an entire sleeve was hanging off the needles. All she'd have to do now was sew the sweater together.

"That looks great, Mom," Jin-Ha said, but she couldn't help thinking of her mother at home, working on a present for her father, while he was out doing something or other, maybe drinking GRAIN BELT beer.

Jin-Ha's mother glanced down at her watch, and worry appeared as a single line on her forehead. Jin-Ha knew she was thinking about her father. Might he still be at the Elks Club? And if so, what did that all mean?

24

The next morning, Jin-Ha gobbled her food while looking at her math book one last time. Her father wasn't up yet. When she heard him in the shower, she bolted from the table to her room.

She waited until two minutes before the bus was supposed to come and then she sprinted through the apartment. Her father was just finishing his coffee.

"Hi, Dad," she said, as she sailed past him.

"Jin-Ha," he said, "did you go out last night?"

Jin-Ha looked at him. He hadn't shaved yet today, and he looked particularly tired. She didn't know what to do about this man, her father. All of a sudden, she felt like she didn't know anything about him.

"Yes," she said tensely. She wanted to say, "Did *you* go out last night?"

"Were you at the library?"

Jin-Ha didn't know what to do. She didn't want to lie, but how to explain?

"Uuuhng," she finally said, a combination of "uh-uh" and "uh-huh" and "ummm." She hoped it would remain deliberately vague. The apartment building shook as the bus rumbled by.

"The bus!" Jin-Ha said in genuine panic. "I have to catch it."

She was out the door.

Once she was at school, there was nothing else to do but concentrate on her math test. No matter what was going on at home, it would have to wait.

Mr. Arneson passed out the test, chuckling slightly under his breath. Today, his necktie sported a candy cane pin that looked rather delicious. At least *he* seemed to be enjoying the Christmas season, Jin-Ha thought. It might be nice to be a teacher, she decided, to be on the other side of the test for a change.

Jin-Ha took a deep breath and started the first problem. It seemed complicated and strange, but when she drew it out, she could see how it worked. She started the second problem, then the third.

The second page was all story problems. She stared and stared at the first one. Then she skipped it and went on to the next one, which was almost exactly like one she'd done last night with Grant—actually, it *was* the same one out of the book! She carefully set up the variables and looked for what she thought the answer should be. If the number five comes up twice as many times in the sequence as the number two . . . it worked—same answer! She solved it and moved on to the next one. Then the next one. And the next.

*　　*　　*

"Tmmmmmmms zup." Jin-Ha felt like she was deep underwater. A voice was pulling her to the surface.

"Time's up," said Mr. Arneson, the candy cane pin on his tie seeming to wink at her. Every space on her test had been filled. That was better than last time, wasn't it? Grant smiled at her, and she smiled back, relieved.

"How was your test?" Deanna asked her first thing at lunch.

"Okay, I think," Jin-Ha said. "Cross your fingers."

"I have them *and* my toes crossed," she said.

"Me, too," said Maggie. "But I'm sure you did great. What do you fabuloso kids think of Christmas shopping after school?"

"Oh, my," Jin-Ha said. "I forgot all about Christmas presents."

After school, the three friends walked downtown.

"First, I need to buy a lump of coal for The Twerp," Maggie declared.

"You aren't really going to do that, are you?" Deanna asked.

"Of course I am. Let's go to Sklaar's Hardware store."

Mr. Sklaar, the store owner, was behind the counter. "What can I do for you, ladies?" he asked.

"I need to buy a lump of coal," Maggie announced.

"Coal?" he said. "The black stuff?"

"Yes, coal."

"Hm," he said, scratching his head. "We don't really

carry coal here. About the best we can do is charcoal briquets left over from the summer."

"Yeah, Maggie, so how much of that is 'char' and how much of it is 'coal'?" queried Deanna.

"That'll have to do," Maggie said. "What else am I going to do—go to a coal mine?"

Mr. Sklaar heaved a dusty bag off the shelf. It said KING'S CHARCOAL on it.

"Oh, I don't need a whole bag," Maggie said.

"How many pieces do you think you'll need?" Mr. Sklaar asked.

"One. No, make it two."

Mr. Sklaar dug out two pieces. They looked like hard, black pillows. Jin-Ha thought it looked like *yun-tan*, the black stuff Koreans used to heat their homes. Mr. Sklaar put the lumps in a little brown bag.

"How much?" asked Maggie, getting out her purse.

"Nothing," he said. "Consider it your Christmas present."

"Really?" Maggie said. "Thank you, Mr. Sklaar!"

As the girls started walking out of the hardware store, Jin-Ha's eye was caught by a little leather holster hanging by the door. She went back to look at it. It was a sheath to be worn on the belt to hold small tools. Her father might like that. He was always complaining how hard it was to keep his tools organized when he was lying under a car.

"A present?" Deanna asked, peering over her shoulder.

"For my dad," Jin-Ha said. "To hold his tools while he's working. I'll have to come back with my money: it's six dollars."

"I have money," Maggie said. "Why don't I buy it and you can pay me back?"

"You don't have to," Jin-Ha said. "I can come back."

"Oh, let her," Deanna said. "She already got a Christmas present, and it was free."

"That was nice of Mr. Sklaar, wasn't it?" said Maggie, handing Jin-Ha the money.

"Yeah, he's so nice, and you're going to turn around and be mean to your little brother," Deanna grumbled. "Some Christmas spirit."

"If you must know," she sighed, "I spent a pretty huge part of my babysitting money buying him that stupid Transformer thing he likes so much. I think he needs the coal, too, so he realizes he's getting a present because it's Christmas and I'm nice, not because he's been a good little boy."

Next, Maggie steered them to Blue Ribbon Sports; she wanted to look for a present for Burt. A sign in its window said WE'RE HAVING A WHALE OF A PRE-CHRISTMAS SALE.

"I could say something to tease you, but I won't," said Deanna, magnanimously.

"Hey, isn't that your dad, Jin-Ha?" Maggie said. Jin-Ha thought she was just trying to distract Deanna. Then she followed Maggie's pointing mitten.

Across the street, her father was walking down the sidewalk with a huge yellow bag in his hand. He had a preoccupied look on his face. Jin-Ha was about to yell to him, but then she changed her mind. What was her father doing downtown in the middle of the day? she suddenly wondered.

"Aren't you going to say hi to him?" Deanna asked.

Jin-Ha ducked into the Blue Ribbon Sports doorway and pulled her friends with her.

"No," she said. "It looks like he's on a secret mission or something. I don't know why he's not at work."

Through the window, they saw her father stuff the yellow bag into his coat and keep on walking down the street.

"Weird," Jin-Ha muttered.

"He's like a reverse shoplifter," Maggie observed. "Most shoplifters pull their stash *out* of their coats when they leave the store."

"Hm" was all Jin-Ha could say. Icy bits of snow were melting on her cheeks. She pulled her hand out of her mitten and bit her pinky fingernail. She used to do that when she was little, whenever she was scared or nervous. Her mother had told her not to because it introduced germs into her mouth. But now, she couldn't help it. She just bit and bit at her fingernail, which tasted of old mitten.

"Jin, you okay?" said Deanna. "Is everything okay at home? Why didn't you say hi to your dad?"

"I don't want to talk about it right now," Jin-Ha said, turning and walking into the store.

"Okay," Deanna said. "But if you want to talk later, just let us know."

"Yeah," Maggie added.

In Blue Ribbon Sports, the clerk was wearing a red Santa hat.

"We have a great sale going on," he told them.

Maggie wanted to get Burt a hockey jersey, but it was too expensive even with the sale, so she settled on a T-shirt.

"Wow, you must be really into him," Deanna commented. "I would think your book would say you're supposed to wait and let the boy buy presents for *you*."

"He's nice," Maggie said with a secret smile. "Look." She pointed to the picture mounted on the wall next to the cash register. "That's Grant Hartwig's brother."

A broad-faced man with piercing blue eyes stared out at them. Even though he was big for his age, Grant still looked like a boy, but the person in the picture looked like a man. He was wearing a V-necked hockey jersey. TO BLUE RIBBON SPORTS, YOURS TRUELY, JOE HARTWIG, CAPTAIN, VARSITY HOCKEY NHS was written in thick black marker pen at the bottom.

"Wow," said Maggie, a little dreamily. "He has nice eyelashes. I heard he might get picked up by the Northstars."

"What a dork," said Deanna, reading the inscription. "As if we didn't all *know* he's on the hockey team, varsity, captain—and that he doesn't know how to spell 'truly.' "

"I wonder if it's hard on Grant, having such a famous brother," Maggie mused. "I know there are some times I just want to kill Jeri for already having gone through junior high and high school doing everything right— Honor Society, band, cheerleader—so there's nothing left for me."

"I doubt Grant even notices," Deanna said. "He seems just as showyoffy as his brother, even if he does help Jin-Ha with her math."

"Grant's not like his brother at all," Jin-Ha said. Both Deanna and Maggie stared at her.

"And what do you know about Grant, pray tell?" asked Maggie.

"Nothing, really," Jin-Ha said quickly. "I just have

this feeling. I mean, sometimes people aren't what they seem at first, right?"

"Maybe you're in love," Maggie teased.

"Oh please," Jin-Ha said. "Would you buy your T-shirt already?"

At home, Jin-Ha carefully wrote: "I owe Maggie $6" on a piece of paper and tacked it on her bulletin board. Her bookshelves were empty now. They looked lonely, like houses where no one lived. She needed to go back to the library and check out some more books.

She went to her closet and pulled down the shoebox that held her special things. Inside she had a baby picture, a wedding picture of her parents, and a picture of her father standing in front of the University of Minnesota, Duluth. Her mother had kept that picture framed in their house back in Korea. Jin-Ha decided she wasn't going to think about the mystery of her father.

After Christmas, I will, she thought.

Underneath that picture was the special envelope. *Please receive many New Year's greetings!* was printed on it in Korean. Inside was her money that her aunt and uncle had sent her last January for lunar new year. When she was in Korea, she would have gone right out and spent it on candy or little notebooks with cute cartoon covers, but she had carefully saved it all this time.

"Jin-Ha," her father said when she returned home. There was no sign of the yellow bag. "Where were you last night?"

Jin-Ha felt a twinge of panic clutch at her stomach. Should she lie and say she was at the library? But she couldn't lie. But how to explain she was at a school dance at the Elks Club?

"I was studying," she said.

"Where?"

"Where were *you?*" she said, suddenly.

Her father frowned and didn't say anything. Jin-Ha kept looking at him.

"It's a secret," he finally said. Jin-Ha saw her mother's head, bent over the stove, straighten up slightly. Even though they were talking in English, Jin-Ha suspected she knew something was up.

"Mine's a secret, too," Jin-Ha said. "I was studying with a friend."

"With Maggie and Deanna?"

"Yes, I was with them," she said, nodding vigorously.

Her father shook his head. Jin-Ha's mother was still staring at them from the kitchen. Then, abruptly, her father walked off to his room.

"Is Dad mad?" Jin-Ha asked her mother, worriedly.

Her mother shrugged. *"Too many secrets in this house,"* she said. Then Jin-Ha regretted speaking so much English to her father, shutting her mother out—but what could she do?

"And don't bite your nails—please!" her mother said. *"In this weather it would be awful to catch the flu."*

Jin-Ha yanked her fingers out of her mouth. She hadn't even realized they were there.

*

"Sorry, class, I haven't had time to grade all your tests—as you saw, this test was three times as long as the other ones."

Mr. Arneson stood in front of them, a Rudolph the

Red-Nosed Reindeer pin attached drunkenly to his tie. It was almost a week since the test.

Jin-Ha groaned. Never before had she wanted to get a test back so badly.

25

After school, the girls went downtown again. Jin-Ha made sure to pay Maggie back before they left. Maggie bought her mother some pretty earrings at Walker's Jewelry *and* the blowdryer with the magic fingers. Deanna bought her mother some perfume that came in a glass bottle shaped like a miniature vase. Jin-Ha would have loved to give her mother any and all of those presents, but she wouldn't have enough money unless she saved her allowance for the next ten years.

But what could she get for her mother, who was so special to her? Her mother didn't like jewelry and things like that, anyway. She didn't blow-dry her hair, or wear perfume or even lipstick! When Jin-Ha pictured her room, it was empty of everything except some books in Korean. She was just not a *thing-y* person.

But then, Jin-Ha got an idea.

"Let's go to the bakery," she said.

"Good idea!" said Deanna. "I'm starving."

The warm air and good smells embraced them like a hug when they walked into Verna's Bakery. A bell over the door tinkled to announce their arrival.

Jin-Ha went to the glass case and found the pastries her mother had been looking at.

"I'll have one of those," Jin-Ha pointed. "And a mug of hot chocolate—extra large and with lots of whipped cream on top."

"Coming right up," the lady said.

"Oh, and could you please cut up the pastry into three pieces?"

The lady nodded.

"Oh, yum," said Maggie as they carried their loot to the table. The hot chocolate looked like a snow-capped mountain, the lady had put so much whipped cream on it. "I've never had one of these before. My mom always buys the eclairs—they're to die for, too."

"Hope you guys don't mind drinking out of the same mug," said Jin-Ha, handing out three spoons.

"I don't have any germs," said Deanna.

"I'm healthy as a horse," said Maggie, scooping off the tip of the whipped cream.

"Merry Christmas," Jin-Ha said. She took a bite of the pastry. It was delicious! And even though the center was filled with some kind of cream filling, not bean paste, it did taste a lot like the ones she and her mother used to get. Maybe Korea and America weren't all that different when you got down to it.

"This is fabuloso," Maggie commented. "Thank you for such a nice Christmas treat."

Deanna licked her lips and carefully used her finger to pick up the crumbs remaining on her side. "But I'm sorry you didn't find a present for your mother," she said.

"Oh," Jin-Ha smiled a secret smile. "But I did. You guys helped me."

"We did?" Deanna and Maggie said together.

"Yeah," Jin-Ha said. "You did."

On the way home, Jin-Ha stopped by the community college. The lady in the office showed her where the brochures were. To Jin-Ha's delight, they had tons of fun classes at night: Spanish language, learning to surf the Web, writing children's books—they even had a class on how to dance the waltz!

"It sounds like your mother might also be interested in our ESL—English as a Second Language—courses," she said, pointing to some brochures in the corner. "Our new classes start in January."

"Thank you," Jin-Ha said, taking plenty of brochures and a registration form. She put them in her bookbag and headed home.

26

The test landed on her desk with a bang, as if it weighed a thousand pounds. Jin-Ha was afraid to look at it; it pulsated strangely as if it was radioactive.

Touching it gingerly, she turned it over.

F!!! F!!! F!!! blared from it in red neon light.

An F? An F? She kept reading: FINAL GRADE: F-MINUS. What could she do? What could she do?

Santa was standing next to her and laughing. No, wait, it was Mr. Arneson in a Santa costume with a beard, but the beard looked real, as if Mr. Arneson had had an operation to *become* Santa Claus.

Then she saw Grant.

"I got an A, I don't know what your problem is, you fem," he said. Then he put his hands on his hips and started laughing a weird Donald-Duck type laugh: "Weahh, weahh, weahh."

Jin-Ha sat up. Her alarm clock was making its peculiar quacking beep. She banged on it to shut it up. It quacked once more, hiccuped, and stopped. Her heart was bouncing in her rib cage like a rubber ball.

It was only a dream. And what a horrible, horrible dream.

*

In the non-dream math class, Mr. Arneson wasn't wearing any Christmas decorations at all for a change. Jin-Ha hoped that was a good sign.

"Okay, class," he said, waving a stack of papers. "I have your tests with your final grades included. Merry Christmas."

Jin-Ha glanced back, and Grant gave her a thumbs-up. Karen Norgaard scowled at both of them.

When Mr. Arneson tossed the test on her desk, it glided to a stop and stayed there, waiting. At least it wasn't pulsating. She pounced on it and turned it over.

98. A. GOOD JOB. A. Good Job. Jin-Ha could hardly believe her eyes.

Good Job. Final Grade: A-minus.

"I got an A!" Jin-Ha said, jumping up from her desk. Standing there, she looked around and saw that the whole class was staring at her. Including Grant, but he was grinning. He gave her another thumbs-up, and raised it higher.

"I got an A, I got an A in math!" Jin-Ha said breathlessly when she burst through the door at home.

Her mother had been sewing a button on the sleeve of her father's new sweater, but she quickly tucked it away when she saw Jin-Ha.

"An A?" her mother said, and she looked puzzled.

"Yeah, an A. Yeeeaaaah!" She proudly handed her mother her test.

"But what about your F?"

"Oh," she said. *"I studied really hard and got an A."*

"But what does A stand for?" her mother asked.

"It's the best grade," Jin-Ha said. *"Ninety to one hundred percent."*

"But F is for fabuloso," said her mother.

Oops, Jin-Ha thought. She had completely forgotten to come up with an explanation. Could she say *A* was for awesome, even better than fabuloso? Would her mother believe that? But then what would *B* stand for? Would she have to keep making up fake explanations for the rest of her life?

"I, uh—" was all she could say.

Her mother was looking at her solemnly.

"Will you please show me your other math tests?" she asked, quietly.

Jin-Ha went to her room. Her mother knew she saved all her tests in her desk.

Reluctantly, she pulled out her tests, a mixture of A's, B-pluses, and the two F's. She brought them to her mother, who looked at each one carefully before setting it down.

"Why does this one and this one have so many red marks on it?" said, holding out the two F tests.

Jin-Ha gulped. She was realizing there was no such thing as a simple lie. A lie crawls somewhere dark to grow into more and more lies, and comes back to haunt you in ways you don't expect.

"I don't know," Jin-Ha said, although she didn't know why she said it, because it, too, sounded like a lie.

Her mother paused. Jin-Ha noticed that the hand holding the tests was shaking a little bit.

"Kim Jin-Ha!" Her mother was angry; she was using her full name.

To Jin-Ha's surprise and horror, her mother began to cry.

"Mom!" Jin-Ha said with alarm. *"What's wrong?"*

But her mother just stood facing her with tears streaming down her face. Jin-Ha didn't know what to do.

"Just because I can't speak English doesn't mean I don't know when my own daughter is trying to fool me," she said. *"Jin-Ha-yah, I depend on you to help me—maybe I depend on you too much. But why do you do this?"*

At the sight of her mother's face, Jin-Ha felt tears rise in her own eyes, but she fought hard to keep them in.

"I didn't mean to fool you—I just tried to hide my bad grades because I was ashamed." Jin-Ha's voice shook. *"I didn't want to disappoint you and Dad, and I figured if I studied hard enough, I could redeem myself—and I did. I got an A in math."*

"We don't care if you fail *at math,"* her mother said. *"The important thing is that you have to tell us the truth AT ALL TIMES. Do you understand?"*

Jin-Ha hung her head and shut her eyes. She wanted to disappear. She wished she'd never been born. She opened her eyes. Still here.

"Do you understand?" her mother repeated.

"Yes," Jin-Ha said finally.

"Do you remember what I said about the new elastic?" her mother said. Jin-Ha nodded solemnly. *"Well, you have to understand that I need more help than you do. You already speak English and have American friends. I don't even know how to buy meat in a market! And here I don't*

*even know if my daughter is doing well or failing at school—
do you know how that makes me feel?"*

Jin-Ha couldn't believe she had hurt her mother so
much. Oh, the truth would never have been this bad!

"I'll never lie to you again," Jin-Ha said. *"I promise. I
promise, really. In fact, I should tell you that I wasn't at
the library the night before the last test."*

Jin-Ha's mother's eyes grew wide, but she didn't say
anything more.

*"I really needed to study for the test, and the only place
my study partner and I could meet was at the junior high
dance, which was at the Elks Club. There were boys and
girls dancing there, but we didn't do any of that. Well, I
danced one dance and part of another, but it was the last
one and we were done studying and Maggie and Deanna
and all these teachers were there. That was it—honest."*

"This math class," her mother said. *"It's been giving
you a lot of worry, hasn't it?"*

"Well, yes," Jin-Ha admitted. *"And I don't like my
teacher very much."*

Jin-Ha was afraid her mother was going to reprimand
her, but instead, she said, *"Why don't you like your
teacher?"*

*"He keeps saying weird things, not just to me. There
was this other girl, Lori Langstrom, he said weird things to,
too, and she dropped out of the class. She was really pretty
and he kept talking about her 'necking,' which kind of
means like kissing. To me he keeps saying things about me
being Japanese and how Japanese are supposed to be natu-
rally good at math and will take over the world or
something."*

Her mother frowned.

"Your teacher said this?"

167

Jin-Ha nodded.

"He sounds like an ignorant man. You know, many years ago, the Japanese would say things like 'All Koreans are stupid,' and use that as an excuse to take over our country and try to destroy Korean culture. For any person to say, 'Such-and-such a people are like this-and-this,' that is the same kind of bad thing. I guess I should have listened harder when your teacher mentioned the Japanese. I'm sorry I didn't."

"That's okay, Mom," Jin-Ha said.

"No, I should be a better mother and listen better. America is a wonderful country, but it has its own problems, too, doesn't it?"

Jin-Ha realized how much better she felt after she'd told her mother everything. It was as if a weight she didn't even know was there was lifted from her shoulders, and she was dumping her pack of lies on the side of the road like dirty snow.

She was curious how her mother would act when her father came home, but then he called to say he would be eating dinner out and had a meeting after that. Jin-Ha saw her mother's eyes darken, as if there might be tears or anger forming, but then she straightened her back and finished cooking, telling Jin-Ha to relax and watch TV.

The two of them ate dinner alone. No matter how much Jin-Ha talked and joked with her mother to cheer her up, it seemed so silent, too silent, without her father there.

27

The day before Christmas, Jin-Ha ran to the bakery early because it would close at three. She bought three of the little pastries and then went to the card store, where she got some wrapping paper. Maybe it was good to be an only child, she thought. It made present shopping a lot easier.

The next morning, of course, was the fun part. Jin-Ha had promised herself that she was going to make a clean start of everything, and last night, she had told her father about her lie. He had been very sad and disappointed, too, but he listened to her story about Mr. Arneson without interrupting. He said he might say something to Mr. Arneson at the next PTA meeting. At the very least, he would most definitely tell him they weren't Japanese and wanted to be thought of as Korean-American.

"So what you did, lying to us, was very bad, Jin-Ha," her father had said. "But what you did in telling us the truth was something very brave. And you worked very, very hard to earn your A in math despite your teacher, so you are very much like Shim Cheong, aren't you?" Jin-Ha basked in this compliment and wondered if her father, in turn, would say something about his strange secrets, but he didn't. No matter what their problems were, Jin-Ha decided, it was going to be Christmas tomorrow, and they would be together.

*

Jin-Ha felt squirmy, like a little kid, as she went to their small living room the next morning. She could already smell the cinnamony Christmas tea that the Hokanssons had given them.

"The tree," Jin-Ha stopped in her tracks and looked up in wonder. *"You decorated the tree!"*

The tree was no longer just a deep green, but green and silver and blue and gold.

"No, Santa Grandfather decorated the tree," her mother said with a smile. Jin-Ha immediately thought of the funny bulge in her coat sleeve.

"Wow, he sure is clever," Jin-Ha said, admiring the graceful silvery ornaments. Some were fashioned from old foil wrappers. Some were made from cans and chrome car parts. There was a gorgeous star at the top, which, when Jin-Ha looked at the back of it, said MAXWELL HOUSE COFFEE—her father must have pounded the can flat and then cut out a nice star shape. The decorations made the whole tree look as if it was winking.

"Give dad his present first," Jin-Ha said, shivering slightly from anticipation as well as from the morning chill. No matter what his secrets might be, right now all she wanted was to see his face when he opened the box with that wonderful sweater. He would know how much Jin-Ha's mother loved him when he saw that.

Her mother handed over the huge box that had once held their *kimchi* pickling jars.

"Oh, you're giving me some jars for Christmas? How practical and thoughtful," said her father, winking.

"Open it, Dad!" Jin-Ha felt she would burst if he delayed a minute longer.

Her father carefully untied the ribbon holding the box together. He peered inside, then peered at Jin-Ha's mother. He finally reached in and lifted out the world's most fabuloso navy sweater.

"Ho," he said, in genuine awe. *"This is the nicest sweater I have ever seen in my life. And the color—it's amazing!"*

"Your favorite color," Jin-Ha piped up. *"Put it on!"*

Jin-Ha's father put on the sweater. It fit him perfectly, sleeves and all.

"Yobo," he said to Jin-Ha's mother, *"how can I thank you? This is so wonderful. You made it yourself?"*

"Who else would make you a sweater?" her mother said. *"You were out of the house enough that I could get it done."*

"Well," her father said, *"you're right. I was out of the house a lot this season, wasn't I?"* He dug out a huge box that he had carefully covered with newspaper. He proffered it to Jin-Ha's mother, who slowly started unwrapping it.

"*Yobo*—" she said, when she saw what was inside.

"What is it, Mom?" Jin-Ha bounced up and down. Her mother reached into the box and pulled out a jewel-pink sweater.

"That's the sweater that was hanging up in That Yarn Cat!" Jin-Ha screamed. Suddenly, she realized. The bag her father had pulled from his jacket was *yellow*.

"*Jin-Ha, let the neighbors sleep.*"

"But, but," Jin-Ha said, "that thing cost a fortune!"

Her father smiled a sly smile. "I made a little extra money calling out bingo numbers at the Elks Club."

"You're a bingo man?" Jin-Ha said unbelievingly. "That was you?"

Her father looked back and nodded. "Who else would it have been?"

Jin-Ha's mother glowed in the sweater. It was so wonderfully soft, and it added a warm pink blush to her cheeks. Jin-Ha remembered how her mother had touched that sweater so longingly when they were in That Yarn Cat. She was always making things for other people, and finally she could have something of her own! Jin-Ha bet she would take the community college classes now—that sweater was far too pretty to keep inside the house.

Jin-Ha's mother plucked at the sleeve. "*I can't believe it,*" she murmured, over and over.

"Here, open mine," Jin-Ha said, handing her mother the wrapped box.

"*No, you open one of yours, first,*" her mother said. Jin-Ha picked up a lumpy present. "From Dad/*Appa*" it said in English and Korean. She tore the paper off.

It was a book. Two books actually: *Black Beauty* and *National Velvet*, stacked on top of each other.

172

"I can't believe it!" Jin-Ha exclaimed. "My own books!"

"National Velvet *is also about horses,*" her father said.

"I've always wanted to read it," Jin-Ha said, hefting the book in her hand. It was going to last her a good long time, through readings and rereadings. "Oh, thank you, Dad!" She got up and gave him a big hug.

"You're getting to be a big girl now, and you've shown us you can be responsible, so why not have a few cherished books of your own?" he said.

"*Jin-Ha-yah, this is for you, too,*" said her mother, handing her a soft, squishy package. Jin-Ha wondered what it could be.

When she opened it, out tumbled some fabuloso-ly soft navy-blue socks and mittens.

"*I had some yarn left over,*" her mother said.

"You are wonderful!" Jin-Ha said. She put them on and sighed, feeling the yarn warming her fingers and toes. She felt warmer immediately. She couldn't wait to get rid of her old mittens, which were unraveling and had a musty smell.

Jin-Ha gave her father his tool belt. He went to the closet and pulled out some tools. "This will come in very handy," he told Jin-Ha, showing her how nicely his screwdrivers and pen knife fit into it. "And I could even hook my gloves to it right here," he said, pointing to a clever leather loop that Jin-Ha hadn't even noticed before.

Then Jin-Ha gave her mother the bag from the bakery.

"*This paper is so pretty,*" she said, looking at the pale green paper printed with silvery stars. "*I want to save it."* She unwrapped the present without tearing the paper and slowly opened the box with the pastries inside. She looked at her daughter.

"These cakes are just like those cakes . . ."

". . . that we used to have at the Nari Bakery back home," Jin-Ha said. *"Well, at our Korean home."*

"And where did you get the money to buy your esteemed parents these lovely presents?" asked her father. *"Do you also have a job at the Elks Club or did you rob a bank?"*

"I used my Lunar New Year money," Jin-Ha said, giggling. *"From last year."*

"You are really such a thoughtful daughter," her mother said.

"And you're a great mom," Jin-Ha said. "And there's more something on top of the box," she said in English.

Jin-Ha's mother looked at the cover of the box and found the brochures taped to the top. She flipped through them and nodded, then carefully put them on top of the folded wrapping paper.

"January," she said. Jin-Ha nodded enthusiastically.

"What about your class, Dad?"

"What class?"

"The one for you to become a teacher."

"Oh, that. I haven't taken it yet—I was just pretending."

"Are you going to?"

"Maybe I can go back to school with your mother," he said, with a twinkle in his eyes.

"I'd like that," said Jin-Ha's mother, a little shyly. She rose and went to the kitchen. She returned with some plates.

"Let's eat these now," she said.

"You and Dad eat them," Jin-Ha said. *"They're for you."*

"You have some, too."

"That's all right, I did already with Maggie and Deanna."

Her mother raised an eyebrow.

"I brought them to the bakery and we all shared one. I wanted to make sure they taste like the cakes we had back in Korea."

Her mother almost looked like she was going to cry. She looked at her husband in his navy sweater and her daughter in her navy socks and mittens. She had to smile instead.

"Isn't this a great Christmas?" Jin-Ha said.

"Yes, this is a great Christmas-oo," her mother said, in *English*.

*

That night, Jin-Ha wore the socks and mittens to bed. She liked sleeping with her hands out of the covers, but they always got cold in the night. Now they were toasty warm, and the yarn was soft, not scratchy like her old mittens. Before she turned off the light, she stared at her bookshelves, where the two books stood like straight, brave soldiers. She had already written *Jin-Ha Kim, 321 W. Lund Street, Apt. 41, Norbuhl, MN 55776* inside the front covers.

So this is Christmas, she thought. Tomorrow she would call up Maggie and Deanna and they would excitedly talk about their presents. She hoped Grant had had a good Christmas, too. When she saw him, she would tell him how telling her parents the truth had made her feel so much better. Maybe if he told his father about his problems with hockey and why he liked to study

math, his dad would understand and they could both
be happy.

Yes, the truth was best.

Happy fabuloso Christmas to all, she murmured to
herself, just as she drifted off to sleep.